Spotted at Lighthouse Bay

ANJ
Press

Pittsburgh

SPOTTED AT LIGHTHOUSE BAY

ANJ Press, First edition. March 2025.

Copyright © 2025 Amelia Addler.

Written by Amelia Addler.

Cover design by Lori Jackson

https://www.lorijacksondesign.com/

Maps by MistyBeee

for the ones we've lost

Recap and Introduction to Spotted at Lighthouse Bay

The fourth book in the Spotted Cottage series...

In the first book in our series, Sheila was the first to take refuge on San Juan Island. It began when she helped Patty, her ex-mother-in-law, save her adorable seaside tea shop. It ended with Sheila falling in love with movie star Russell Westwood – and a wild plan to rehabilitate and release Lottie, the captive orca, back into San Juan's waters in a specialized sea pen.

Eliza and Mackenzie, Sheila's daughters, also discovered love on the island. While Mackenzie is busy helping Russell run his new charity, Eliza stays at the tea shop, perfecting recipes and taking flights with pilot boyfriend Joey.

Sheila's younger sister Adelaide didn't plan on falling in love when she moved to the island. She figured her time had passed, and her only desire was to find a place to piece her life back together after her divorce.

It's too bad that fate had other plans...

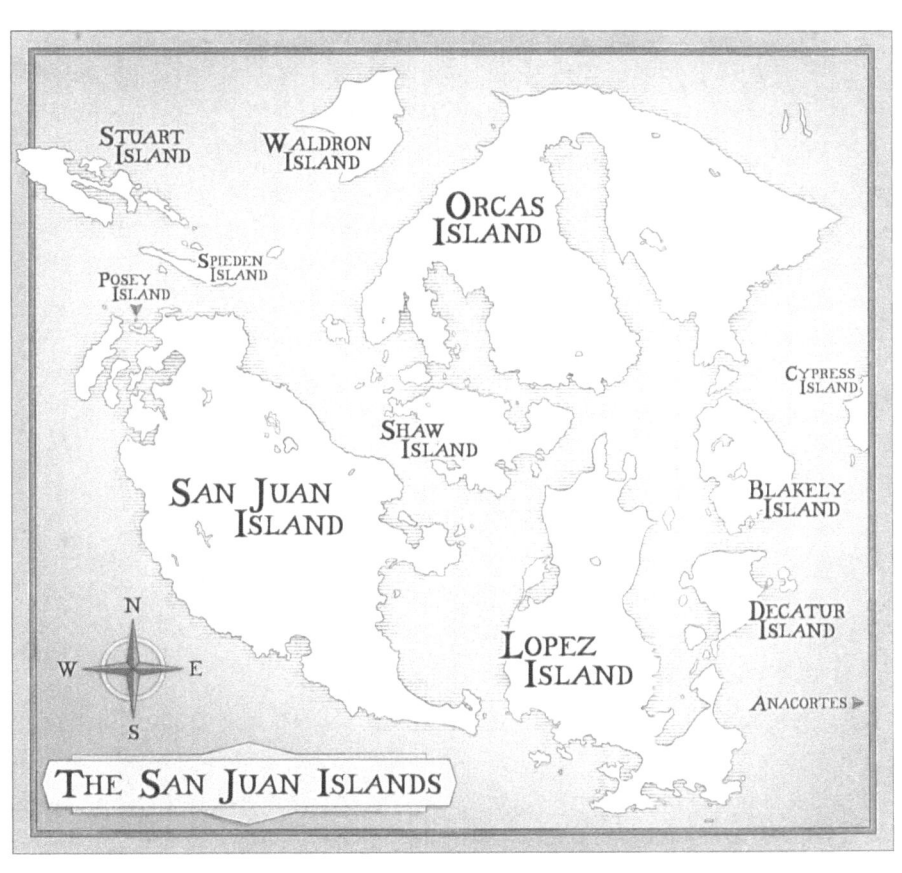

STUART ISLAND

WALDRON ISLAND

ORCAS ISLAND

SPIEDEN ISLAND

POSEY ISLAND

CYPRESS ISLAND

SHAW ISLAND

SAN JUAN ISLAND

BLAKELY ISLAND

DECATUR ISLAND

N
W · E
S

LOPEZ ISLAND

ANACORTES ▶

THE SAN JUAN ISLANDS

One

It was a boundlessly blue-skied September, the fall after her divorce, and Adelaide had no idea how she'd ended up on that beach.

She sat cross-legged, facing the water, a notepad in her lap and an empty wine bottle propped in the sand at her elbow. A breeze lifted the pile of crumpled papers next to her and she swatted them down.

Why was this so hard? The book made it sound effortless. It was literally step one: write down your greatest fear.

Her sister Sheila hadn't recommended the book to her. Addy had found it on a shelf, its muted cover calling to her with a single word from the title, a siren call: **MIDLIFE.**

Surely by forty-eight she should be able to admit her greatest fear. If not her greatest, at least the top three. It rolled around in her head for days. She was sure once she focused on the question, she would figure it out with ease.

Yet here she sat, with nothing but the birds above her and what might have been a harbor seal peeking its nose above the water from afar. The cool air stung her lungs, but she breathed deeply anyway, savoring the pure ocean air.

She stared at the notepad, down at the scrawled list of things that had already happened to her. Divorce. Losing the beacon of her life, her father. Being laid off from the university. Her mother walking out on them as kids. The bittersweet moment of her daughter taking off to college, starting her own adventure.

Addy's handwriting was wild and looped, like she was racing toward the answer, but all she had was a list of abandonments. Her greatest fear wasn't being abandoned. If anything, she was a pro at getting left behind. A gold medalist – or at least silver.

The edges of her greatest fear were stark in her mind, but she couldn't see the fear itself. It sat perched in the darkness, watching over her with black eyes.

She looked up. The sea glittered under the sun, and the trees in the distance stood like bursts of green joy. Two months on San Juan Island and she'd still managed not to take it for granted. The cool, clean air. The scent of pine needles on her early morning walks. The soft lapping of waves on the rocky shore.

Her fear, the dogged thing, didn't feel welcome to join.

The sun pressed into her skin and she closed her eyes. It should be easy. It should be obvious. Addy's life was full of fear. Full of worries – worrying about doing the wrong thing or making the wrong choice, being punished by ending up in the wrong place.

All her life, she believed if she lived within the prickling bounds of her fears, lived within the rules, life would reward her. The Bad Things wouldn't happen, and she would be happy and whole.

She opened her eyes. None of it worked. Even after following every rule, and spending years tossing in twisted covers with a racing heart, the Bad Things happened anyway.

She'd lost people, relationships. She'd lost security.

She'd lost herself.

Yet how could she complain? Here she was, on this beautiful day, staring at a vast and endless ocean. She was *alive*. Those fried nerves felt it with every kiss of breeze.

Death didn't scare her. Not exactly. Statistically, she had almost an entire new lifetime ahead of her – another four decades.

Her heart dropped and sweat sprung beneath her sweater. Her best years were behind her. What would she do with another forty years?

What would she do with another forty years *alone?*

The beast in her mind cackled a low, rumbling laugh, and finally she got her glimpse. She snatched the pen into her hand, the words dancing across the page like a bird dipping its wings into the water. *Will anyone ever love me again?*

There it was. Her fear wasn't as simple as her best years passing her by. Her fear shouted that everyone else saw it, too. Wife, mother, and then what? There was nothing left to love. Only something to be discarded.

She was *used up*.

The fear, disgusting as it was, lost half its power by being named. Her hands moved swiftly, the salted air buoying in her chest as she folded the paper into a square. She shoved it into the bottle, then pressed in the cork.

Addy walked to the water's edge, the low waves touching the tips of her boots, and drew her arm back. The bottle rose above her head and she snapped it forward, a crack ringing out from her shoulder.

"Ack!"

The bottle splashed in front of her as Addy grasped her shoulder.

Aggravating an old shoulder injury. That should've been her greatest fear. She wouldn't be able to lift her arm for a month. Maybe two.

"What on earth are you doing? Littering for fun?"

Addy spun around. That voice was too high to be real. It couldn't possibly be... "Mom?"

"The one and only."

New fear unlocked.

A grin spread across her mother's face, red lipstick on her front tooth. "Why are you throwing trash into the ocean? I know I taught you better than that."

Addy blinked. Six years ago, her mom had showed up at Christmas without warning and complained there were no gifts for her. She looked remarkably the same, though her lipstick had changed from a maroon red to a lighter pink.

"I'm cleaning, actually." Addy bent down and picked up the bottle. Her right arm hung at her side, aching.

"No you're not! I watched you throw that."

"What are you doing here, Mom?"

"What kind of welcome is that for your mother?" She stepped back, her lips pressed into a scowl. "I thought you'd be happy to see me."

She sighed, tucking the bottle under her arm. "Of course I'm happy to see you. I'm just surprised."

"Well, I didn't expect *you* to be here, either. Where's Shane?"

The throbbing in her shoulder intensified. Addy used her left arm as a sling. "We got a divorce. I called you."

"I can't be expected to remember every little thing," she said with a wave of her hand. "Did you know things are rocky with my boyfriend too?"

"What boyfriend?"

"Then, worst of all, someone stole *all* of my savings! Right out from under me!"

"What? Who?"

"Scam artists! I was trying to save the house for me and Lawrence. He'd fallen behind on payments, and when I tried to help, they took *everything*! What am I supposed to do? You're going to have to help me."

"I –"

"Oh my, is that your new man? A bit young for you, don't you think?"

Her mother had never been all there, but now she really must have lost it. "Mom, what are you talking about?"

"That fella right there. He's got his eyes on you. Don't play coy."

She pointed and Addy turned. Walking down the hill from the tea shop was a dark-haired man in jeans and a black shirt. The wind blew against the shirt, outlining a hard chest. His eyes were covered by sunglasses, and his face was pinched in a scowl.

Addy laughed. "That's not my boyfriend. I don't know who that is."

"Well," she dropped her voice, "he's headed right for you."

Two

H e scanned the area. Sand, sea. No boats on the water that could reach them. A perfectly boring scene, and two women looking up at him.

"Adelaide Ashbourne?" Rick asked when he reached them.

The younger one raised her eyebrows. "Yes?"

She matched the pictures he'd gotten. Rick put his hand forward. "I'm Rick Hayle from IronClad Elite."

"Uh, nice to meet you."

Her hand was small in his. She pulled it away quickly.

The older woman stepped forward. "I'm Adelaide's mom. You can call me Marilyn."

His eyes darted between them. "Mrs. Ashbourne, I trust your husband Shane updated you on the situation?"

Marilyn spoke again. "*Ex*-husband Shane. She's single."

"Okay, Mom," Adelaide said. She sighed. "No, I haven't spoken to him. Is he okay?"

He should have known. No last-minute assignment would come without complications. "Yes, but there is a concern about a case he's presiding over and I've been hired to provide personal security for the duration of the case. Is there somewhere we can speak in private?"

"There's nothing you can't say in front of me," Marilyn said, chin raised.

He turned to Adelaide. Her right arm was cradled in her left, a wine bottle tucked close to her chest. She nodded past him. "We can talk over some tea."

Marilyn narrowed her eyes and walked past him. Adelaide joined her, and Rick followed at a distance.

"I don't want you to get scammed like I did," Marilyn said, loudly, looking over her shoulder. "You can't just trust everyone, you know. I got scammed because I'm a good person."

The wind filled his ears, rendering Adelaide's response inaudible.

They stepped into the tea shop with a jingle of the door. The young woman at the counter smiled when she saw him.

"Oh good! You found her."

Rick nodded. "I did. Thank you for your help."

She'd already shown him around the tea shop when he'd stepped in a few minutes prior. Still, he went to every room and checked the bathroom. All clear.

Marilyn put her hands up. "Eliza! I thought you were your mom for a second."

Eliza flashed a smile. "Grandma. Hi."

"I'd love a pot of tea," she continued, lowering herself into a chair with an *oof*. "Any black tea is fine; you know I'm not picky. And fresh cream."

Eliza nodded. "Of course. Anything for you, Aunt Addy? And Mister..."

"You can call me Rick." He hadn't come for a tea party. "I'm fine, thank you."

"Call Shane," Marilyn said, glancing at Rick from the corner of her eye. "I want to hear what he has to say."

"He left me a voicemail yesterday..." Adelaide pulled out her phone. "I haven't listened to it yet."

"Well, you've got to listen to it!" barked Marilyn. "What were you thinking?"

"I didn't think it was important, Mom," Adelaide said, voice low.

"Well, of course it is. Look at this guy," Marilyn whispered. Loudly.

"I can wait outside if you'd prefer," Rick said.

"No." Marilyn held up a finger. "I don't want you sneaking around. You sit."

He didn't move from his spot by the door. "I'll be here."

"Excuse me," Adelaide said, stepping behind the swinging door leading to the kitchen.

Marilyn sat back, arms crossed over her chest. She zeroed her eyes in on him. "Do you think you could do me a favor?"

He stared at her. "It would depend on the favor."

"Could you track someone down?" She leaned forward. "You know, like a criminal?"

Rick raised an eyebrow. "That's not what I do."

"Hm." She waved a hand. "What is it you do, then?"

"I provide personal protection to those experiencing threats to their safety."

"Was it Shane, then? Who threatened Adelaide?"

He took a deep breath, looked at her, then back to the swinging door. Adelaide emerged a moment later.

"Sorry about that," she said, walking toward him. "It's not that I didn't believe you. I've just never been in a situation like this before."

"I understand," Rick said. "It's wise to be cautious. I'm sorry you weren't aware before my arrival."

"Why do you need a bodyguard, Adelaide? What did you do?"

"I'm not sure. Shane didn't answer, but he left a voicemail saying to expect someone." She cleared her throat. "Am I really in danger?"

"What do you expect him to say? Of course he'll say you are." Marilyn jerked a thumb toward Rick. "Otherwise, he doesn't get paid!"

"*Mom.*"

Nothing from the file he'd gotten had indicated this woman lived with her elderly mother. If it had, he might've turned it down. "I assure you, you're in good hands. Out of an abundance of caution, the firm involved in the lawsuit agreed to pay a third party for your protection."

"Well, if *that* isn't fishy," Marilyn continued. "How do we know they're not the ones that made the threat?"

"I'm an army veteran with a decade of experience in personal security. I have no association with the firm involved in the lawsuit and I can assure you your daughter is in good hands, Marilyn."

"Please stop insulting my bodyguard, Mom," Adelaide said, shaking her head. She flashed a smile. "Do you want to take a seat?"

Better to stay by the door. "I'm fine, thank you."

She set the wine bottle down and took off her coat, gingerly bracing that right arm.

Eliza returned with a tray of tea.

"I've got our London Fog blend for you, Grandma," she said, setting down a tea pot and cup.

Marilyn scrunched her nose. "Is that lavender I smell?"

"Yes, and I've got some sugar cookies as well."

"You'll like it," Adelaide said.

Marilyn sighed. "I suppose I'll get used to it."

"Is there anything you can tell me about the threat?" Adelaide asked.

Rick cleared his throat. It was enough that her file was barren. Now he had to work through the awkward details. This was what he got for signing up for a job no one else wanted.

"A brick was thrown through your ex-husband's window."

Adelaide gasped, her hand going to her mouth. "A brick? Is he okay?"

"No one was injured. Following that, a second brick came through with a message that read, 'Your wife won't survive the wrong decision. Choose wisely.'"

"It said 'your wife?'" Adelaide asked, her head cocked to the side. "What is this case about?"

"I'm sorry. I don't know."

"Okay." Adelaide nodded. "How afraid should I be?"

"The attack didn't seem like the work of a professional," Rick continued. "Of course, we can never be sure of a threat, but I would not label you as a high risk."

"But I need a bodyguard?" Adelaide said, eyebrows knitted close.

"I was hired out of an abundance of caution," he repeated.

"Sounds scammy to me," Marilyn said under her breath.

Another older woman emerged from the back room.

For a small tea shop, it was filling up. He needed to lock that back door.

"Excuse me," the woman said, "but I caught the end of this." Her hands were behind her back, tying an apron string. "I'm Patty, the owner of this tea shop. If you are who you're claiming to be, you should be able to provide identification."

"Of course." He reached into his coat pocket and handed her his driver's license, military ID, and the credential card IronClad Elite had rushed to print for him.

"IronClad Elite." Patty narrowed her eyes. "This is your company?"

"Not my company, no," Rick said. "They hired me to fill this position. It was an emergency contract."

She raised an eyebrow. "You're not a regular?"

"No."

Patty frowned, handing his ID back. "If they're so elite, why don't they have staff trained and ready at all times?"

Rick glanced at Adelaide. She was seated, cradling her arm, her expression unreadable. Maybe in shock. "I can't speak to that. I've worked personal security in the past and was called in by a friend at the company."

"Well," Patty said slowly, "I hope you're good enough to take care of our Adelaide."

"Okay, Patty. Thank you." Adelaide stood, walking closer to him. "Rick, I'm not entirely sure what's going on, but thank you for the information and...welcome to the mad house."

He nodded. "Thank you. Glad to be here."

Three

This whole thing was ridiculous. Addy didn't need a bodyguard. No one was going to come all the way to San Juan Island to attack her, and if they tried to, she could take care of herself. She wasn't some doe-eyed damsel in distress.

The one embarrassing thing that proved she wasn't quite so savvy was her not asking Rick for his credentials. It felt too rude! Patty, on the other hand, had no qualms.

Maybe Patty could be her bodyguard.

Addy's phone rang and she quickly pulled it out of her pocket. It was Shane. She rushed to the kitchen before answering.

"Hey, Shane."

"Adelaide, hi."

She bit her lip. He'd never used her full name during their nineteen years of marriage. It was always *honey*, or *boo-boo*, or *Lay-Lay*. It wasn't until the end he'd transitioned to calling her *Addy*.

It was a standard nickname for her, but hearing it from him was jarring. She'd noticed it immediately. She knew in her heart then that it was over, but it took her another two years to accept it.

"What's going on, Shane? There's a man here claiming to be my bodyguard."

He sighed. "I was hoping I would get to talk to you before he arrived. Things happened so quickly."

"Are you okay? I heard something about a brick?"

"Yeah, that wasn't great. It came through the living room window."

She had no idea what his new house looked like. How strange that was. "Oh."

"No one was hurt. It's a high-profile case. I can't talk about it, but you might've seen it in the news."

"I haven't."

"A company is suing the government for the right to donate to politicians."

"Isn't there a law limiting political spending?" At least in Canada, where Shane was a judge.

Being back in the US, she was surprised by the endless political ads. One had such a frightening voiceover that it had made Patty's golden retriever Derby jump and leave the room.

Shane cleared his throat. "It's complicated and, as you can imagine, people are fired up on both sides. There's an argument that it violates the Canadian Charter of Rights and Freedoms."

Addy raised an eyebrow. "This is a company arguing that? I doubt the average Canadian citizen wants companies to have more influence over politicians."

"Adelaide, I can't talk about this with you."

Oh. Adelaide now.

She sucked in a breath. "Okay, sorry."

"We're not sure who made the threat, but the company generously offered to pay for personal security for you."

"Why are they threatening *me?*" she asked.

He was quiet for a beat. "That's the thing. We're not entirely sure they meant you."

"I thought the note said 'your wife might not survive,' or something."

"Right, well." Shane cleared his throat. "I'm seeing someone. She lives with me. Whoever was watching me, I think they were talking about her, but we can't be sure."

"Oh." Her voice, the traitor, went up an octave. "Of course. Then I don't need a bodyguard."

"Better safe than sorry. That way I can feel safe to make the right decision."

Oh, right. This was about him. Absolving *him* of guilt. Making sure *he* could work unencumbered. "How long is this going to take?"

"No more than a few weeks, hopefully."

"A few weeks!" She caught herself and lowered her voice. "I'm not going to have this guy following me around for weeks, Shane."

"You don't have a choice."

Her mother's voice carried through the door, followed by Sheila's. It might be shouting or laughter; she wasn't sure.

"I have to go," Shane said, "but I can understand why you are having a lot of emotions about this."

He was talking to her like she was a mental patient. He'd picked up some key phrases in couple's therapy. Empty words without feeling, in his case. In her case, an emptied box of tissues at every session.

"It's fine," Addy said, "I have to go too."

She ended the call and pushed the kitchen door open. Sheila stood over their mother, hands on her hips. Sheila's boyfriend Russell stood back by Rick, watching the scene unfold.

"Why are you being like this?" Sheila barked.

"Sheila," Addy said, placing a gentle hand on her elbow. "If anyone walks in, they're going to think you're trying to fight an old lady."

"Maybe I am," Sheila muttered under her breath.

Addy led her back to Russell, who stood by the door, his face flat, his eyes watching them all.

He had to think they were all nutters. Her most of all.

Marilyn sat in her chair, her purse in her lap, her eyes round. "I'm just trying to enjoy my tea."

"You said it tasted like poison," Sheila said over her shoulder.

"I said I've had better." Marilyn picked up her teacup and put it to her lips. "But I've traveled all over the world—what do you expect? For me to lie to spare your feelings?"

Eliza forced a smile. "Can I get you something else, Grandma?"

"No, no." Marilyn tipped the cup back before setting it down with a clatter. "Don't worry about me. I make do."

Rick's dark figure floated into the corner of Addy's vision. She jumped.

"Is everything okay?" he asked.

"Yes, it's fine," Addy said. "This is my sister, Sheila."

"Hello, Sheila."

Sheila ripped her elbow out of Addy's grasp. "Who's that?"

"That's Rick," Addy said, trying not to smile.

"Who is Rick?" Sheila demanded.

"My bodyguard." Addy turned toward him. "I spoke to Shane and –"

Sheila cut her off. "How do you know Shane?"

Big sisters, always so quick to demand answers. This was getting out of hand.

Addy's shoulders dropped. "Sheila, come with me. Let's talk."

She led her into the kitchen. The door swung open and Rick stepped in behind her.

"I just needed to confirm there's no door in here."

Sheila's jaw dropped. "Excuse me, Rick! Get out of here!"

He disappeared behind the door and Addy covered her mouth with her hand.

It was wrong to laugh, but if she didn't she would lose her mind. "He's my bodyguard, Sheila."

"Your *what?* Did I walk into another dimension, Addy? What is going on?!"

With a deep breath, Addy told her about the court case, the threat, and Patty interrogating Rick.

"Patty came to get me," Sheila said, "and she didn't even mention Rick. She said Mom is here and looking for money."

"I'm not sure what the story is with the money yet."

"Let me tell you something," Sheila said, voice low. "The last time I let Mom stay in my house was when I was selling it. She refused to leave and I had to pack up all of her stuff on closing day and move it out myself! I am *not* letting her stay with us. Not at Patty's cottage, and certainly not at Russell's house. If you let her in, you will never be rid of her."

Addy bit her lip. "Tell me how you really feel."

Sheila let out a huff. "That is how I really feel. I know she's our mom, but you can't get sucked in. She takes and takes and takes."

"I know, Sheila. Don't worry. We'll find somewhere for her to stay."

She sighed, leaning against the counter. "Tell me more about this bodyguard. What was the threat?"

Addy shrugged. "Something about Shane's wife being in trouble if he made the wrong decision."

"What?" Sheila scowled. "That doesn't make sense."

"Shane seemed to think it was more likely about his new live-in girlfriend, not me. They still sent someone to watch over me until the case is over."

Sheila's mouth fell open. "Oh, Addy. I'm sorry."

"It's fine," she said, voice too high again. "We're not together anymore. It's not like I was holding out hope we'd rekindle our love affair."

"But still. It stinks."

It did stink, but Addy wasn't going to dwell on it.

Patty pushed her way into the kitchen. "I couldn't help but overhear what you two were talking about."

"Overhear? You never hear anything when I'm trying to talk to you," Sheila said.

Patty waved a rag at her. "It's because you always try to talk to me when I'm washing dishes. Don't you worry, Adelaide. I know plenty of eligible bachelors on the island and I'm a very successful matchmaker."

Sheila and Addy met eyes. "Oh?"

"You never would have met Russell if it weren't for me, Sheila," Patty said. "You're welcome."

Sheila laughed. "You're right. You're a matchmaker."

Patty grinned. "Thank you."

Addy had no interest in being matched. She had no interest in a bodyguard, or in Shane's love life, or –

"There's a note in this bottle!" Marilyn called out. "Here let me – hang on, I can do it. I just need to grip it right..."

No! That was not happening. Not on top of everything else.

Addy kicked the kitchen door open, napkins fluttering in her wake.

Four

When they'd told him Adelaide's sister was dating Russell Westwood, Rick had had his concerns. Celebrities brought drama, but surprisingly, Russell seemed to be the most normal one in the bunch. Or, at least, the quietest.

Marilyn's face reddened, her long nails clutching at the bottle's cork. Rick leaned against the wall, arms crossed, as the swinging door came to life yet again.

Adelaide stood in the opening, her eyes narrowed on her mother, her chest heaving with quick, short breaths.

The muscles in his shoulders tensed. Had something happened?

"I can't believe how good it's stuck in there!" Marilyn said. She held the bottle up to Rick. "You've got muscles. Maybe you can help me."

"That's not yours!" Adelaide said, stepping forward.

Marilyn shrugged. "It's not yours, either."

"I found it," Adelaide countered.

"Don't be selfish. My goodness." Marilyn shook the bottle, the paper inside making a soft clink. "Can't we all enjoy whatever fun the tide brought in?"

Adelaide looked up, her eyes scanning the room. "I just..."

Patty and Eliza were dealing with a customer at the front of the store. No one seemed threatening, but something wasn't right about this bottle.

Rick reached out and pulled it from Marilyn's hand. "Let me try."

Marilyn turned, a smirk on her face. "See? Some people have manners."

"Some people weren't raised by wolves," Sheila said in a low voice.

Rick tucked the bottle under his arm. "On second thought, this could be a threat to Adelaide. I'll have to investigate it."

"A threat!" Marilyn let out a tut. "You're being ridiculous. Don't spoil the fun."

Adelaide took a breath and looked away.

So it was the bottle.

Rick shook his head. "It won't be any fun if there's an incendiary device inside."

Russell laughed. "You're a serious guy, Rick."

"That's what they pay me for."

"I'm Russell Westwood," he said, extending a handshake. "I'm not a serious guy, but sometimes I play one on TV."

Rick smiled. "I've seen your movies. They're good."

"Thanks. I appreciate that."

More important than the movies, Rick hadn't heard any negative stories about Russell. That was rare, especially as famous as he was.

"Rick is my new bodyguard," Adelaide said. "Shane is on a big case and there were some threats."

"I already told Russell about it," Marilyn said, waving a hand.

Russell cleared his throat. "You're welcome to stay with me, Rick. I've got an open room right next to Addy's. You can keep an eye on her."

"What about me, Russell?" Marilyn dropped her hands onto the table, her rings making a clank. "I'm practically your mother-in-law and you haven't offered me a room yet."

"Hm, I wouldn't go *that* far," Patty said, scooting by with a tray on her hip.

"We're not married, and you have no right to demand to stay in Russell's house," Sheila said. "Or, for that matter, Patty's either. We're full."

"I came here to tell you I've been robbed and all you can think about is technicalities. So what if your boyfriend didn't give you a ring?" Marilyn shook her head. "You're fifty years old, Sheila. It's –"

"I'm fifty-one, Mom." Sheila crossed her arms over her chest. "Didn't you bring anything for my birthday?"

Marilyn sighed. "How could I? I keep telling you, I was robbed!"

Adelaide took a seat next to her. "What happened, Mom?"

"Finally, someone's paying attention." She sat back in her seat, resting her hands on the table in front of her. "I was living with Lawrence for almost a year."

"Who's Lawrence?" Sheila asked.

"My boyfriend, of course."

"Of course." Sheila rolled her eyes.

Russell leaned over and said in a low voice, "I'm going to stay out of the crossfire."

Rick nodded. This was of no interest to him, but he'd been held hostage by duller exchanges.

Marilyn went on. "He was having problems paying his mortgage, and he found a company that would help him with it."

Sheila raised an eyebrow. "Help him how?"

"I'm not sure of the details, but they worked out a deal so he could use the equity in the house."

"Probably a sale-leaseback," Sheila said. "I know where this scheme is going. They bought the house from him and then rented it out at twice the price."

"It's not a scheme," Marilyn snapped. "Two nice young men came to the house and explained it to both of us, and he signed up. He got a good payment for it, too. Paid for a twenty-one-day cruise for the both of us."

"I'm sure he got a payment," Sheila said. "For a tenth of what his house was worth. Then they kept bumping up his rent until he couldn't pay, right?"

"We don't discuss money. It's crass and ruins the romance." Marilyn turned back to Adelaide. "I knew he was having some trouble, but the men came around the house again. They said if I paid off the remainder balance of the house, it would be all sorted. So I went to the bank –"

Adelaide groaned. "No, Mom, you didn't."

"I went to the bank and took out fifty thousand dollars."

"Fifty thousand!" Sheila's mouth dropped open. "How did you get that much money?"

"It's my life savings, Sheila. I had to go to five different banks because none of them had that much cash on hand."

Sheila's hands completely covered her face.

"I gathered it all up, met with the men, and signed the paperwork."

"What paperwork?" Adelaide asked, her voice muffled behind her hand. "Do you have a copy of it?"

"They were supposed to send it to me, but a week later, we got an eviction notice. I couldn't reach them, and I started to wonder if they'd stolen that money from me!"

"We can't help you, Mom." Sheila shook her head. "Some guys off the street took you for a ride, and you gave them all of your money."

"They weren't off the street! They work for the company. Key House or something."

"Do you have their names?" asked Russell. "Maybe we can talk to them and figure out what's going on."

"Was it House Key?" Marilyn tapped her chin. "I would ask Lawrence, but his phone is disconnected. We're not talking anyway. I came here to get help from you girls before it's too late."

"That money is gone." Sheila clapped her hands together. "I don't know what to tell you."

"It can't be gone! I bought the house, Sheila."

"No, you didn't. How could you buy it for fifty thousand dollars? Didn't he get more than that for his payment?"

"Yes, I suppose he did." Her lips curved into a frown. "This is what I get for trying to do good. Believe me, it's the last time I'll do anything good."

"We'll figure something out," Adelaide said gently. "Give me a second. I'll make some calls."

She stood, walking to the front door, and Rick followed. Outside, his footsteps crunched in the gravel and Adelaide spun, jumping when she saw him.

"You don't have to follow me," she said.

"Actually, I do." He pulled the wine bottle out from under his arm and handed it to her. "I think this is yours."

She accepted it. "Thanks."

He nodded. "Pretend I'm not here."

"That seems rude," she said slowly. "I'm only going to make some calls. I need to find my mom a place to stay."

"You don't have to explain yourself to me." He bowed his head slightly. "I'm just here to watch your back."

She cleared her throat. "Right. Okay, thanks."

Her eyes fell and she walked a short distance to a nearby bench, taking a seat.

He stood behind her, scanning the area. There was no one nearby, and no way for anyone to approach without him seeing them first.

Rick relaxed his shoulders and looked up. The sky was a sea of blue, cloudless and endless.

He remembered that from when he was a kid, coming to visit his cousin, Cody, out west. The sky was always blue, the sun always shining.

It was too much sun for Rick. It had suited Cody's character, though. He had been like a sun, always giving off that warm glow.

Until it had stopped.

The tea shop door opened and Rick snapped his attention over. It was Sheila, moving fast, her eyes narrowed and fists at her sides. She shot him a glance before walking over to Adelaide.

He had to smile. At least he wouldn't be bored.

Five

"I don't like this one bit," Sheila announced, hands on her hips.

Addy leaned away, covering her phone with her hand. "Okay, thank you," she said before ending the call.

She sighed and turned to her sister. "I don't either, Sheila, but what are we supposed to do? Tell our mother 'Good luck, you're on your own?'"

"That's what she did to us when we were kids. Why do we owe her anything?"

"We don't owe her anything," Addy said slowly. "But I know I couldn't live with myself if I didn't help her. I'm going to do what I can."

Sheila put her hand over her mouth and groaned. "I know. I wouldn't feel good either, but she just got here and I'm already sick of her."

It felt like someone had tightened a band around her head. Their mother could be incredibly charming and, at times, make Addy forget her grievances. Today had not been one of those times.

Instead, she had to remind herself that her mother was a flawed—but not unlovable—person. She'd had an extraordinarily hard start in life and, because of that, she struggled and hurt those around her. Her harms were never malicious or planned. Her mother had always had to look out for herself because no one had looked out for her when she was young and defenseless. It made her comically selfish at times.

Other times less comically, but it helped to imagine her as a scared girl and not a pushy old woman.

Addy rubbed the back of her neck, trying to fix the image in her mind's eye. "I know, but I have good news. I called around town and there's an opening at the Piano Key Inn."

"Patty knows the owners," Sheila said.

"So do I." Addy grinned. "Patty introduced us a few weeks ago when they came for tea. They're going to give us a discount for Mom to stay in a suite."

"Look at you!" Sheila poked her in the shoulder. "Making friends everywhere you go."

Addy shrunk down, her hand flying to her shoulder. "*Ah.*"

"Did that hurt?" Sheila shot a look back at Rick. "I don't need your bodyguard coming after me."

"It wasn't you. It's an old tendonitis injury flaring up."

Addy looked up and Rick was at her side. He'd somehow managed to walk silently on the gravel.

"Everything okay?" he asked.

"Yes." She paused. "I'm sorry about all this confusion, Rick. I'm afraid I've been rude and I'm sorry. Things will calm down after I get my mom settled. Why don't you go to Russell's and get set up?"

"You haven't been rude. I apologize that you weren't made aware of my coming. I know it can seem unnatural at first, but I won't be leaving your side for the time being."

"Question for you," Sheila said loudly. "Do you have a gun?"

"Why do you ask?" Rick put his hands on his hips. "Do you need to borrow it?"

"I'm just curious," Sheila said with a shrug.

"Sheila –" Addy warned.

"What? Don't you want to know? Like, how does this all work?"

"I have everything I need to protect your sister," Rick said.

Sheila stared at him, and when he didn't say anything else, she took a step back. "Okay then."

If Shane could see them now, he'd say Sheila was butting her nose where it didn't belong and Addy was being overly accommodating. He'd scold her for asking too many questions and tell her to go with the flow.

Which flow she was supposed to embrace right now, she wasn't sure.

Addy glanced between them, then clapped her hands together. "All right. I'm going to take Mom into town so she can get settled in her room and stop upsetting everyone."

"I'm happy to drive," Rick said.

"No, that's okay. You can go and unpack."

"I insist. I have a bulletproof vehicle."

Addy stared at him. She realized her mouth was open.

"So no one can shoot at Mom?" Sheila mused. "That might come in handy."

Addy shot her a look. "Sheila."

"I also carry a first aid kit," Rick said, nodding at her. "I can make a sling for your shoulder."

Was she being that obvious? "Thanks, but it's nothing."

"Come on, go with him," Sheila said. "Maybe if you have a sling, I'll remember not to jab you again."

"I should go get Mom," Addy said, casting her eyes toward the tea shop.

It was loud and windy out here, but surely even louder inside with Patty left toe-to-toe with her mom.

Sheila raised an eyebrow. "Getting her out of the tea shop will be my only contribution today. Go!"

"All right. Thanks."

"I'm in the parking lot," Rick said with a nod.

Addy led the way, up the hill, past the tea shop. A black SUV sat gleaming in the sunlight.

"This looks like something from a spy movie." she said.

He unlocked the car and opened the trunk. "I'll admit it's a bit on the nose, but it's top of the line. Makes things simple."

She leaned in. The seats were black leather. The windows were tinted black, and the inside of the doors reflected back at her like bottomless pools. "Is it yours?"

He shook his head. "No. IronClad Elite provided it as part of the contract."

The trunk was spotless. Rick opened a black suitcase and lifted a large bandage out of a compartment. "May I?"

"It's really not a big deal. It flares up now and again," she said.

"I understand, but you've been holding that arm since we met. It can't be comfortable."

She looked down. Apparently she'd been obvious. Did that make her look like prey to any predators? Did anyone out there even know she existed? Know that she'd been part of Shane's past, the part he'd hastily tossed away?

He gently lifted her arm and pressed it into her abdomen. "Hold that here."

His hands were large, and his skin was rough against hers, but his touch was as light as a hummingbird. Goosebumps rippled across her skin.

He looped the bandage under her arm, tying it behind her neck. "How does that feel?"

She let her arm fall into the support. The ache eased, dissipating for the first time since she'd failed to throw the wine bottle. "Much better."

"It should hold up until we can get something more durable."

"Thank you, Rick."

"Don't leave without me!" Marilyn yelled, walking out of the tea shop.

Sheila was close behind her, pulling a large, boxy suitcase over the rocky path.

Addy took a deep breath. "Did you hear the good news, Mom?"

"Yes! I'm delighted!" Marilyn walked to the passenger door and opened it. "Finally, some luxury. You know, in my younger years, I rode in cars like this all the time. Limousines, town cars. I dated a man who wouldn't let me lift a finger. Always sent his driver for me, like I was a queen."

A queen of what, Addy had no idea. Collecting boyfriends, maybe.

"Tomorrow I can try to talk to Lawrence and figure out what company you were working with," Addy said.

"Thank you, Adelaide. I always know I can go to you when I need help." She placed a hand on Addy's cheek and patted it.

Addy turned to get the suitcase, but Rick was already loading it into the trunk.

"Oh, thank you," she said.

How many times was she going to have to thank this guy? She was a broken record, mumbling and muttering like a servant to her mother's queen.

He nodded, opening the back passenger door for her. Using her good arm, she pulled herself up and slipped onto the leather seat.

"I could get used to this," Marilyn said, the front seat humming as she adjusted it backward into Addy's legs.

Addy scooted to the other seat. "You've changed your tune. I thought you said Rick couldn't be trusted."

"The man has a nice car, Adelaide. That's something I wouldn't take for granted."

Addy sighed and rolled her eyes. There was no point in arguing. It would only leave her doubting herself and feeling guilty. Best to smile, nod, and get through the day.

. . .

It took four hours to get her mom set up at the inn. First, they got her luggage into her room, then she announced she was hungry. They popped into the restaurant next door, and during the meal she asked if they'd take her grocery shopping. Then, she wanted Addy to show her where the bus stop was, in case she decided to do some sightseeing. After that, she wanted to see if there was a nail salon in town and what their prices were.

Catering to her mom was one thing, but doing it in front of a stranger made Addy feel exposed.

Mercifully, Rick didn't betray any annoyance. He only spoke when spoken to – which wasn't often, as her mom had a lot to say about her recent travels and schemes. In some ways, it was easier having him there than her ex-husband.

Shane used to sigh, and roll his eyes, and make faces. It was a point of contention when her mother showed up, and though Addy did her best to keep the peace, it wasn't always possible. Short of kicking her out while engaging a screaming match, he would never have been happy.

When they were finally walking back to the car without Marilyn, Rick spoke up. "Shouldn't we get your arm sling?"

She sighed. "I'm sure you're exhausted. I can get it another time."

"I'm fine. There's a pharmacy just there." He nodded, squinting into the sun.

They walked to the pharmacy and she picked out a sling.

"So," Addy said, shoving the sling into her purse. "where are you from?"

"Kansas."

"Ah." She nodded. "I've been to Topeka. It's lovely."

"It is."

They got back to the car, Rick looking over his shoulder as he opened the door for her.

"Thank you."

He looped around the back

"Russell's driveway is right before the tea shop."

He nodded.

She looked out the window. As much as Addy wanted to say something useful, her mind was blank. For the first moment that day, Addy missed her mother. She had filled the silence.

"Do you mind if I turn on the radio?" she asked.

He shook his head. "It's all yours."

She clicked it on, and a song her daughter Riley liked rang out. She closed her eyes for a moment, the stress of the last few hours leaving her body as she sank into the seat.

Six

G ravel crunched under the tires as he pulled into the driveway. Rick stopped the car and Adelaide sat up with a quick breath.

"Sorry," she said. "I think I dozed off for a second."

Must be nice, sleeping so easily. "No problem."

He shut off the engine and opened the door, the cool evening air rushing in. A two-story house towered above with tall windows and knotted wooden accents. Trees bowed overhead, the hush of the wind blowing through the leaves, the ocean a whisper in the distance.

For this moment, he was suspended at the edge of the world. This was perfection. Peace was in reach...

The car door slammed and he snapped back to reality. He should've opened it for her.

"Home sweet home," she said, taking a deep breath. She paused, looking at him. "Where were you going to stay if Russell didn't have room?"

"I've got a sleeping bag," he said, walking to the trunk.

Her brows shot up. "That can't be comfortable. Sleeping on the ground?"

"On the ground, under the stars." He paused. At least he had a view then, being up all night. "Depends how you look at it."

"Optimistic." She touched her pointer finger to her nose. "I like that, Rick. We can always use more positive attitudes around here."

The last time he'd been optimistic was when he'd signed up for the army at eighteen. Rick kept it to himself. Life was a game of knowing when to speak up – or, more aptly, knowing how often silence was the right choice.

"Sure."

He opened the back and pulled out two duffel bags. Normally he traveled lighter than this, but they'd told him to be ready to stay a while.

Adelaide stared at him for a moment, then walked to the front door. "Hopefully this will be more comfortable, even if you can't watch the stars. In exchange you'll get a toilet, and heat, and mandatory games of charades every night."

If she was kidding, she didn't betray a smile. He followed her, eyeing the property.

She pushed the front door and he walked into the open space. The kitchen was clean lines and granite. Straight ahead was a wall of glass with a view of the sea. A telescope and soft couches framed the view.

Rick had never wanted anything to do with fame. It seemed to seep into people's minds and destroy whatever humanity they had, one ego burst at a time.

But this? Was there a way to get something like this without selling out?

Sheila and Russell sat at the kitchen island, Sheila's face lighting up when she saw them. "You're finally back! What took you so long?"

Adelaide smiled. "You know how it goes. Mom was hungry. She needed groceries. Then she wanted to know how the bus worked, in case we can't drive her where she needs to go. And she needed to know the price of a manicure."

"Uh huh," Sheila said. "Then she wanted to tell you about her horoscope?"

It had actually been about a dream she kept having, but close enough.

Adelaide laughed. "Pretty much."

"Terrific." Sheila shook her head. "I almost felt guilty I wasn't nicer to her. *Almost*."

"That's the cycle," Adelaide said with a sigh. "I managed not to snap at her, so I'll take that as a win."

"Incredible. Let me get you a glass of wine."

Russell stood, arm outstretched. "Can I help you with your bags, Rick?"

"I'm all right, thanks," Rick said. "You have a beautiful home. I appreciate you letting me stay here."

Russell waved a hand. "Please. You're more than welcome. As long as Adelaide is in trouble, you're the guest of honor."

"I'm not in trouble," Adelaide called out, empty wine glass in hand. "I'm in *danger*. Allegedly."

"In danger," Russell corrected. He frowned. "Thinking about it, I'm not going to kick you out if you manage to keep Addy away from danger, though, so…"

"What he's trying to say is that you're a welcome guest, Rick," Sheila shouted over her shoulder. "Can I get you something to drink?"

Rick shook his head. "I'm all right, thanks."

"Would you like the tour?" Russell asked.

"I would, yes." Rick scanned the room. A bowl of oranges on the counter. Family pictures on the walls. Not nearly gaudy enough for a Hollywood star. "Do you have a security system?"

"I do, but to be honest, I never figured out how to use it."

Sheila walked over. "Russell! You told me you got it working."

"I thought I did, but turns out I was just flipping through the settings every night."

She shook her head. "Unbelievable."

"We'll need to address that," Rick said. "I'll also need to walk around the property to see if there are any vulnerabilities."

Sheila crossed her arms over her chest. "The biggest vulnerability is Russell forgetting to close the door. Last week I came over and it was wide open. Blowing in the wind."

Russell laughed. "That was bad, but in my defense, Patty had told me Eliza had just pulled a cinnamon apple cake out of the oven and she needed someone to try it."

"You left the door open because of cake?"

Russell shook his head. "I left the door open because of *Patty*."

Seemed fair. Though Marilyn ruined every quiet moment with her demands and musings, Patty was the one Rick needed to watch. She was the gravitas granny.

He looked down. Was that what this job would end up being? Assessing grandma threat levels?

"Should we do the walk-through now?" Rick asked.

"Sure." Russell nodded. "We'll drop your bags off and start upstairs."

"Do I have to come along for the walk-through?" Adelaide asked.

Rick looked at her. She was perched on a stool at the kitchen island, a glass of white wine in her hand. He didn't want to disturb her, but... "It shouldn't take long."

She nodded, smiling brightly. "Okay!"

"I'm coming too!" Sheila said, rushing over. "I don't want to be left out."

Rick followed Russell up the stairs and dropped his bags in his room. He had a private bathroom and a window with a view of the ocean through the trees. Above the bed, a deep window cut through the ceiling. He'd still have a view of the stars.

They wove through each room, checking window locks and dark corners while Adelaide and Sheila chatted behind them. Outside, they walked the property line down to the shoreline. Sheila made a video call to Russell's daughter, Mia, and asked Rick to say hello.

"I've never met a bodyguard before!" Mia said, waving and smiling.

He nodded. "Hello."

He never knew what to say when people commented on him being a bodyguard. In truth, it wasn't so different from being in the army. Hurry up and wait. Boredom randomly interrupted by terror.

Hopefully there wouldn't be any terror this time. He needed this job to stay easy. Enough of a challenge to keep him sharp, but not enough to rouse his nerves. The confidence boost might be all he needed to get back to normal. To himself.

If anyone suspected him of being less than capable, they didn't betray their thoughts. The trio followed Rick as he walked on, inspecting the dock on Russell's property, then returning inside to set up the security system.

It was more advanced than he'd expected, and impressive in a way. Russell didn't know what he had going for him.

He was busy fiddling with the keypad when Sheila offered him a glass of wine.

Rick didn't look up from the security keypad. "I don't drink on the job."

Or ever, but that wasn't for her to know or for him to explain. So much of life was knowing what to keep private. That was what most people were missing. Talking too much, telling everyone their problems. It was probably half the reason Marilyn got scammed. The lady couldn't stand birds getting a chance to be louder than she was.

He shook his head, forcing himself to focus. Even if this job wasn't high stakes, he couldn't keep letting his mind wander. He had been hired for a reason, and he was going to do it to his own standard.

Once the alarm was set up, he took a seat on the couch. Sheila asked him to join their game of cards, but he declined. It was never a good idea to get too comfortable with the clients. They should get comfortable with him – view him as part of the scenery, even – but he always needed to be on guard.

When Adelaide announced she was retiring for the night, Rick walked her upstairs and cleared her room before shutting the door.

Inside his own room, he opened the window. Clean, crisp air blew in. He closed his eyes, breathing deep breaths. A good end to a long day.

Rick broke away from the window and took a shower. It was a fancy thing, white marble and glass walls. The shower head sprinkled above him like a summer rain, relaxing his muscles.

After the shower, he laid in bed and stared at the ceiling. The stars had been blocked by clouds.

The next morning, he woke with a start when he heard Adelaide's shower kick on. He got dressed quickly and stood outside her bedroom door.

She screamed when she opened it and walked into him.

"Sorry," he said. "I didn't mean to surprise you."

"No, I'm sorry. I never knew it was so easy to sneak up on me until now." She smoothed her hair with her hand. "How'd you sleep?"

He could only remember one nightmare, and he'd gotten at least three hours. "Pretty well. And you?"

"I had a weird dream about someone following me. I guess I'm more creeped out by the threat than I realized." She rubbed the back of her head. "Would you like some breakfast?"

"I'm fine, thanks."

The company had provided him with a credit card for his expenses. He'd grab something on the way or eat a protein bar from his bag.

She turned, walking down the stairs. "I make a mean breakfast sandwich. If I made one and left it in front of you, would you leave it there? Or would you eat it?"

"Uh..."

"Would you waste a sandwich, Rick?" She leaned in, forehead creased. "Or do you have some dietary restrictions I should know about?"

"No, but –"

She spun. "One sandwich, coming up!"

He sighed and followed her to the kitchen. She had four slices of bread in the toaster and a frying pan heating up within seconds.

Rick stood to the side, arms hanging uselessly at his sides. That wouldn't do. He found the coffee pot and dumped out the old filter and grounds. A rolled bag of coffee stood next to it. He opened it, the sweet aroma filling the air.

"Mugs are in there," Addy said, pointing to the cupboard.

He pulled out four. Presumably Russell would wake up soon, and Sheila might show up, too.

If no one else wanted coffee, he could drink the entire pot himself. Caffeine had no effect on him. The insomnia left him chronically exhausted. At this point, his body didn't want to sleep. It would be unfamiliar, too much like a threat.

Russell came down just as Adelaide finished the sandwiches, and Sheila popped through the front door. Their appearance plunged him into a parallel universe. Russell burst into song and grabbed Sheila by the hands, swinging her around.

Like last night during the card game, he caught a glimpse into a life he hadn't chosen, where people enjoyed breakfast together and meant it when they laughed. Adelaide watched them, cheering, serving up fried egg sandwich after fried egg sandwich.

Rick's was the first. The edges of the egg were slightly browned and perfectly crispy. Melted cheese oozed over the edges of toast. Adelaide lined his plate with fresh strawberries and blueberries.

It beat a dry protein bar, and he didn't have to sing or dance for his.

Once Russell finished his song, he released Sheila to settle in with Adelaide and babble a mile a minute. From what Rick could pick up on, their mother had already begun requests for the day, but Adelaide had staved her off by telling her they were going to Bellingham to talk to Lawrence about the missing money.

"Mom's being very cagey about it all," Adelaide said, taking a sip of coffee. "She keeps telling me not to mention her missing money to him."

"She's up to something." Sheila shook her head. "I'm not looking forward to figuring out what that is."

Rick got up to pour a second cup of coffee as the front door opened. A young man walked in.

Rick moved quickly, stepping in front of Adelaide. "Can I help you?"

"Oh, hi. I'm Joey, Russell's pilot." He stopped and smiled a half smile. "Are you the bodyguard?"

"I am." He lowered his shoulders and stepped back.

"Sorry. I forgot to mention," Russell said, clearing his throat. "Joey has the other bedroom upstairs. He flies a seaplane for me. We have a project on Stuart Island."

"Have you heard about Lottie the whale?" Sheila asked.

Rick shook his head.

"She's an orca who was captured in these waters decades ago. It's a long story, but we're bringing her back."

Rick stared at her. "To live with you?"

Maybe Russell wasn't as down to earth as he seemed, wanting a whale as a pet.

Russell laughed, a bit of cheese flying from his mouth. He wiped it away, coughing. "Adelaide will have to catch you up. We've got a sea pen built for her to retire into. To let her step away from her life performing."

Rick grunted. "Lucky whale."

"It shouldn't cause any problems for you," Russell said, then stopped. "Just keep in mind there might be contractors or veterinarians looking for me."

"Don't shoot anyone," Sheila added, smiling.

"I won't." Rick walked back to the coffee pot and finished filling his mug.

Joey grabbed a bagel and ate it while chatting. Rick finished his coffee and got the plates into the dishwasher.

"You don't need to clean up," Adelaide hissed, trying to beat him to the last empty mug.

"You cooked. It's only fair."

She stopped trying to pull the mug from his hand and sighed. "Fine."

They grabbed their coats and Joey led them down to the beach. The seaplane floated at the end of the dock, white paint blinding in the sun.

Another plus to being a star. Convenience.

"Thanks for taking us, Joey," Adelaide said. "Have things been busy?"

"Very. Not to complain," he said, stooping to untie the plane. "I like it. But I'll have to pick you up about an hour or two after I drop you off. Is that okay?"

"Of course! I appreciate it." She turned to Rick. "Do you want to sit up front?"

"No, I'm all right."

"I insist! You have to get the best views on your first flight over the islands."

Before he could protest, she had climbed into the back seat of the plane.

She wasn't one for listening, that Adelaide. He got up front, put on a headset, and within minutes, they were in the air, soaring over the little green islands dotting the deep waters.

Joey was another talker. Was that a requirement for living on the island? Blabbing your life story?

Rick still liked it here, but he'd have to move to one of the less populated islands. Get a few acres. It would be just him and the water every night. Maybe a few dogs. He could go weeks without seeing another person.

He wasn't supposed to isolate like that, though. It made the nightmares worse. Among other things...

Maybe a cat, too.

They landed in Bellingham and Joey taxied to a dock. "I'll text you when I'm heading back, but I don't expect more than two hours, tops."

"Thanks, Joey!" Adelaide stepped onto the dock.

Rick followed with a thud. A man brushed past them, carrying a fishing rod over his shoulder. Another walked past with a crab trap.

Adelaide put a hand to her forehead to block the sun. "Mia sent a text that she's here. She has a blue sedan."

He'd made note of the car as they were landing. Mia stepped out of the driver's seat and waved.

Sometimes he noticed too many things. He knew it was Mia, but he still had to pretend. "Is that her?"

"Oh yes, there she is!"

Adelaide raised an arm and waved. Two men encircled Mia, blocking her from view. She pushed one off, but he pressed back in, looping his arm around her shoulders as the other filmed with his phone.

Rick's stomach tightened. Flipped. Sparks ran up his arms, and numbness filled his fingertips. He forced himself to take a breath.

No, not now. He couldn't fall apart at the first sign of trouble.

He shut his eyes. Deep breaths. He could see these guys were a threat. Everyone could. He had to react.

The churn in his gut fizzled to a quiver. He opened his eyes. Mia was still ensnarled.

Rick broke into a sprint.

Seven

It was like something out of a movie. If Addy hadn't seen it with her own eyes, she wouldn't have believed it.

By the time Rick reached Mia, one of the guys had lifted her into the air.

"Look!" he yelled. "I caught the woman who single-handedly ruined the Apex Universe!"

She squirmed away and fell to the ground. In one swift motion, Rick grabbed both men by their shirts, picked them up, and tossed them to either side like paper dolls. They hit the pavement with a skid, groaning.

Addy rushed to Mia and squatted down next to her. "Are you okay?"

She stood, swiping at her knees and smoothing her hair. Her cheeks glowed. "Yes, I'm fine. It's okay."

One of the guys scrambled backward on his hands and knees. "Dude, what is your problem?"

Still laying on the ground, hands up, the other said, "Yeah, what the –"

"Do you want to try that again?" Rick said, his voice slow and steady. "Or do you want to leave?"

"We were just –"

Rick took a step toward him. He flinched.

"You were just leaving." Rick knelt and picked up the dropped cell phone, never breaking his stare. "Right?"

The guy stood, joining his friend. "That's my phone."

"Not anymore," Rick said. "Get out of here."

Both men hesitated before quickly turning and walking off, casting looks over their shoulders once they were across the street.

Addy stood next to Mia, gripping Mia's hand. She let go.

Rick turned to Mia. "Are you all right? Do you want to call the police?"

"No, no police." She shook her head. "I'm fine. It's nothing."

"It was assault." He handed her the phone. "I think he was recording you. It should be easy to prove if you want to press charges."

"I don't want to prove anything," she said, pushing the phone back into his hand.

"What was that about, Mia?" Addy asked. She took the phone from Rick's hand. "Did you know those guys?"

She shook her head. "It's about this superhero movie I was in. I had a small role. It's really dumb. I don't want to cause any trouble."

A crack ran across the center of the phone's screen, splintering to the edges. The video floated dimly behind it. It was frozen on Mia's grimacing face, her head bowed in a headlock, her hair flipped and mangled.

Heat flashed out from the center of Addy's chest, reddening her neck. When she was younger, she'd let herself get pushed around, too. She knew the feeling. She knew the fear of speaking up.

Thank goodness she wasn't young anymore.

Addy turned to Mia. "How about this? I'll send the video to myself, then delete it from this phone. If anything comes up, we'll have the evidence, but otherwise, no one has to know about it."

Mia's eyes darted to Addy, then across the street, then to Rick. "I don't know. Sure, that's fine." She rubbed her elbow. "It's really okay, though."

"Of course it's okay." Addy smiled. She texted the video to herself, then deleted it from the phone. She went the extra step to delete it from the trash folder, too. "What should I do with this?"

Rick stuck out his hand. "I'll take care of it."

She handed it to him, and he drew his arm back and chucked it across the street. It cascaded into the water with a plop. "Have a nice day, boys!"

The guys stood, watching them from across the street. Like a pair of Muppets, they scowled in unison.

Mia and Addy burst into laughter. A half smile even crossed Rick's face. He had the slightest hint of a dimple, which looked out of place on his rugged face.

"Thanks for that," Mia said. She took a deep breath. "I'm going to get back into my car before they get any more ideas."

"Good idea," Adelaide said, jogging around the car to get into the passenger seat.

They piled inside, slamming doors.

"Sorry about that. People usually just try to get a picture. Those were the first guys who took it too far." Mia said, clearing her throat. "It's nice to meet both of you in person!"

"It's so nice to meet you too, Mia!" Adelaide beamed at her. She looked so much like her mother, but there was a touch of Russell, too. Mostly in the eyes.

"You should consider carrying pepper spray," Rick said, leaning forward.

Mia laughed. "You're a good bodyguard, Rick. I don't need it!" She turned to Addy. "The motel Lawrence is staying in is pretty close. Shall we?"

"Yes, please." Addy's phone dinged. It was a text from her mom.

Don't like the boats tooting in the harbor. Is this all the time? Can you call someone about it?

She stared, then put it back in her pocket. Best not to engage.

It was a short drive to the motel. Mia pulled into the parking lot and Addy noted that the motel had two levels, with painted aluminum siding and a black, wire handrail along the second level.

"This isn't nice," Addy said in a low voice.

Rick chuckled, looking through his window. "You think?"

She smiled to herself. It was the first time she'd made him laugh.

They walked to door number six. Addy knocked.

"Coming!" a voice called out.

The door creaked open, revealing an older man in a white button up shirt and black slacks.

He grinned. "For a second there, I thought you were Marilyn!" He stuffed his hand into hers. "Spitting image of her."

It was the first time she'd gotten that. Addy wasn't going to take it personally. "Hi, Lawrence. I'm Adelaide."

"Come in, come in! How are you? Can I get you something to drink?"

They all declined, but he fussed with an electric teapot balanced on a nightstand anyway. "How's Marilyn? You'll have to tell her I miss her."

"She's good." Addy paused. He didn't seem like a man who wasn't trying to keep in touch with her mother. "I'll pass your message along to her."

"Please, sit," he said, motioning to the neatly made bed.

Addy, Rick and Mia sat down. The bed sagged under their weight, with Rick in the center.

"I hope you're hungry!" Lawrence picked up a paper plate and handed it to Addy.

The Ritz crackers nearly spilled over, some topped with hummus or thick cut yellow cheese, some with a pink spread and dill.

Addy balanced the plate before any escaped, selecting a cheese cracker before passing it on.

"She's a real firecracker, your mom," Lawrence said, beaming. "Why would she want to stay with me when I didn't have anything? I don't blame her." He shook his head. "Oh, but I love her. I still love her. You have to know that."

Addy glanced at Rick. He was staring at the plate. She cleared her throat, and he passed it to Mia without picking anything up.

"I have no doubt, Lawrence," Addy said with what she hoped was a gentle tone.

The creases on his face broke into a smile. "I never meant to lose the house. This whole mess…"

"I'm hoping I can help both of you," Addy said. "My mom tried to tell me about the deal you made for your house, but she didn't know the details. Do you have the paperwork?"

"Yes!" He disappeared behind a door, reappearing with a manila folder. His hands shook as he handed it over. "I've got everything from Flex Knock here."

"Flex Knock," Addy repeated, opening the folder. There was a stack of papers, all legalese.

The tea kettle steamed and beeped. Lawrence talked on. Addy flipped through the papers, making sure to look up and nod occasionally.

Sheila had told her what to look for, and when she reached the end of the first stack, it was clear it was just what Sheila thought it was: a sale-leaseback. Flex Knock had bought the home from Lawrence and paid him a lump sum of fifty-eight thousand dollars.

Fifty-eight thousand for a home worth at least three hundred thousand!

The catch was with the lease. Lawrence was supposed to be able to pay back the fifty-eight thousand plus interest, along with rent, and eventually reclaim his home. There was a rental agreement that followed, spelling out the cost of renting the home during that period. In small, complicated language, it said rent was fixed for only the first three months, then it was to be increased "by market value."

Hence the stack of overdue notices that followed. The company had increased Lawrence's rent from one thousand dollars the first three months to twenty-three hundred in month four. Then twenty-five hundred by month six, and three thousand a month by the end of the year.

Criminal.

"Do you have the names of the people you worked with for this? Or who first came to the house?" Addy asked.

"Afraid not. It was always someone different. Though I did see the guys I first talked to walking around the neighborhood again last week. I went back to get a memorial stone from my garden. Luckily, they didn't see me." He spun around with a tin in his hands. "Would you like a cookie?"

"That would be lovely, thank you." Addy had to get out of there before her heart broke in half. She took a butter cookie and popped it into her mouth. "Thank you so much for your help. I'm going to try and talk to the people at the company and figure something out."

"Thank you, sweet Adelaide, you're a lifesaver. Please send Marilyn my love."

She forced a smile. "I will."

Adelaide stood, and Rick and Mia shot to their feet.

"Nice meeting you," Mia said, first one to the door.

Rick nodded. "Take care."

They walked through the parking lot, silent as their feet plodded against the pavement. Once the car doors slammed shut, Mia spoke first.

"I feel so bad for Lawrence!"

Addy sighed. "Me too. My mom left out the little detail that she'd broken up with him."

Mia gasped. "What? Why?"

"My mother..." Adelaide bowed her head forward. The pulsing intensified. "She's a complicated woman."

Addy pulled out her phone and navigated to Flex Knock's website. There wasn't much there. No site listing with salespeople. The business card had the name of the CEO: Cliff Atkin.

There was, at least, a phone number. She dialed out on speakerphone, and the ringing echoed endlessly in the car.

After a minute, she gave up and ended the call. "Weird," she said. "I guess I can't avoid talking to my mom about this. Do you mind if I call her now?"

Mia shook her head. "I'm invested. It's like a soap opera."

"Ha. It is." Addy hit call again. Her mom answered quickly.

"Adelaide, you need to find me a quieter place to stay," she said, breathless. "These boats are too loud and I can't sleep."

"If you stay outside of town, you won't be able to walk anywhere," she said.

"Then you'll have to drive me!"

One problem at a time. "Mom, I just spoke to Lawrence. Why didn't you tell me you'd broken up with him?"

"Does it matter?"

"Sort of, yeah." She sighed. "What else aren't you telling me?"

"Nothing!" she squeaked, voice sky-high.

Adelaide knew this game. She waited.

"Well," her mom finally said, "I don't see what difference it makes, but..."

Addy kept her voice steady. "Yes?"

"I suppose when I got my money out of the bank, we weren't *fully* together anymore, but I didn't want to leave the house! They told me I could take over the payments."

"Who told you that?"

She sighed. "The guys. I told you, the ones who came to the house."

Ah, the mysterious guys who came to the house. Of course. "They told you that you could take over as a renter?"

"No, they *specifically* said I'd be buying it."

There it was. Addy shot a look at Mia, who had covered her mouth with her hand.

"So you broke up with Lawrence, then tried to buy the house out from under him, and the mystery guys took your money and disappeared?"

"I wouldn't put it that way, but technically, yes. If you're being ungenerous."

"Got it. Okay Mom, I need to find out more about Flex Knock."

"Flex Knock! That was it! Yes, great work, Adelaide." She cleared her throat. "I needed to talk to you about my neighbor here, too. I think she plays a harmonica at night and it's *extremely* irritating."

"Uh huh." She looked down, glancing ever so quickly at Rick. His eyes were hidden behind black sunglasses, his head slowly scanning around the car.

If she didn't know any better, she'd think he was tuning all of this out somehow.

At least he was polite.

Eight

Someone across the street was looking at her. Mia knew that squinting, focused glance. They were early in the process of recognizing her.

Maybe she could prevent it from happening.

Adelaide was still talking to her mom. She mouthed a "Sorry!"

Mia shook her head, smiled, and compressed herself down into the car seat. If only she could slip a little lower...

"Look alive," Rick said. "We've got company."

Bang, bang, bang.

Mia jumped as the glass of her window shook. How had he gotten here so fast?

She rolled down the window. "Yes?"

"Are you Mia Westwood?"

She nodded. "I am."

"I can't believe it! I'm a writer for the Bellingham Star. Movies and entertainment."

Was it a full moon today? "Oh, hi. Nice to meet you."

His mouth was frozen in a stiff, toothy grin. "Do you mind if I ask you a few questions?"

Mia looked over her shoulder at Adelaide. She was pulling her phone away from her ear. "Mom, I've got to go. We'll talk later."

"Um," Mia turned back to the man at her window. "Sure."

"Thanks so much. First, what was it like to work in the Apex Universe?"

"It was really great, and I appreciated the opportunity to... be a part of it." She was terrible at this. What was she even trying to say?

"What do you think about some people saying they wished your character had been killed off sooner?"

She sucked in a breath. His teeth were still in her face, their false friendliness making her brain short circuit.

It was jarring – the mismatch between his smile and the intensity of his eyes.

"Get out of here!" Adelaide said, leaning over the center console. "Don't you have better things to do?"

"This is my job," he shot back, leaning into the car.

"Well, you're bad at it." Adelaide waved a hand at him. "And you're getting nowhere in life. Mia, close the window. We're leaving."

He slammed his hand down next to her head. Mia jumped.

"I'm not done yet," he snapped.

Adelaide reached over and plucked his fingers off the car, one by one. "Yes. You. Are!"

He shouted, clutching his hand to his chest. Adelaide hit the button and the window climbed back up, sealing them in from the sounds of the street.

Adelaide let out a huff. "The nerve of these people is unbelievable. Are you okay, Mia?"

"Oh yeah, I'm fine." She nodded, swallowing the lump in her throat.

"How about we go somewhere else to regroup?"

Why hadn't she thought of that? If she sat here any longer, Rick would have to leap out of the back of the car and throw that guy in the air, too. It was mortifying that she couldn't stand up for herself. She was an embarrassment.

A quiver rose in her throat as she put the car into drive.

"What is with people?" Adelaide said as they pulled away. "They act like they're entitled to your attention. Why is it always the ones who have never done anything who have opinions about everyone else?"

Mia nodded.

Adelaide went on. "People probably think because your mom and dad are famous actors that they can say anything to you."

That was exactly what it was. Even before she had been in any movies herself, Mia would get cornered by people who wanted her to know something about her mom and dad – either their opinions on their divorce, or ranting that their movies were bad, or asking to be invited to Thanksgiving.

It was one thing to get accosted by a pair of jerks at the dock. Now, not even an hour later, someone else? Was this going to be the rest of her life? She'd been a fool to think she could pull off being in a superhero movie. It was totally unbelievable. She was an embarrassment to the entire family.

Inside Mia's chest, a balloon popped and a sob exploded out of her mouth.

Adelaide put a hand on her shoulder. "Let's stop. Pull in right here."

Mia's vision blurred, shaking with tears. She blinked them away and turned into a parking lot, stopping in the first spot.

"I'm sorry," Mia said, her voice shaking.

"You don't have to be sorry," Adelaide said gently. "You've had three strangers come after you today."

"Two physical assaults, one verbal," Rick noted.

Crying was only more shameful, but the more she tried to stop, the more the tears forced themselves out.

Mia buried her face in her hands and sobbed. Adelaide rubbed her shoulder, her voice soothing and calm, and slipped tissues into her hand.

After four loud nose blows, Mia was able to regain her composure.

"I'm so sorry," she sniffed. "I'm not normally like this."

"I'm sure you're not normally attacked by strangers, either." Adelaide shook her head. "Is this all about the same movie?"

"A movie I ruined." Mia shook her head. "They're right. I was terrible in it. I'm a terrible actress."

"I'm sure that's not true."

She looked up, locking eyes with Adelaide. "It is."

Rick cleared his throat. "Would anyone like a drink? Looks like they have coffee here. Tea." He leaned, looking through the windshield. "Baked goods."

Adelaide handed Mia another tissue. "Yes, that'd be great. Thanks, Rick."

He snapped his seat belt and popped the door open. "I'll be here, in sight, so don't worry."

Mia looked up. There was a window for people to walk up and order. He wouldn't be more than ten feet from the car.

"We'll be fine," Adelaide said.

He shut the car door and disappeared.

Mia looked down at the pile of tissues in her lap. She was embarrassing all of them. No wonder he'd wanted to get out of there.

"I'll be honest, Mia. I didn't see the movie. I'm not into superhero things, but even if you were terrible, it doesn't give anyone the right to treat you that way."

"It was so bad. I really did ruin it."

"Sounds like they killed your character off, though." Adelaide smiled. "You can't cause any more damage."

A laugh sputtered out of her. "That's true."

"And who cares? It's a movie. You're a person. A real person, not someone to pick up and yell at in public. It's ridiculous."

"Yeah." Mia took a deep breath. It was shaky, but she wasn't going to burst into tears again. "I'm sorry. I know you're in a hurry."

"Don't worry about that. Whatever trouble my mom's gotten herself into will still be there tomorrow."

Mia sat in the quiet for a moment. "You know, it's not even that people are being nasty about it."

Adelaide leaned in. "What is it, then?"

"My mom helped me get the job. She thinks I'm talented, that if I don't do movies, I'm wasting a huge opportunity."

"Is that what you want to do?" Adelaide asked.

The car door popped open as Rick returned with a drink carrier in his hands. "I wasn't sure what you wanted, so I got a cappuccino, something called an oat milk latte, a strawberry banana smoothie, and an iced tea."

Mia finally felt composed enough to look at him. She turned around. "That's an interesting mix."

Adelaide laughed. "Positively inspired, Rick."

"Just following orders." He picked up the pink smoothie. White whipped cream floated on top in a heavenly stack. "I see you eyeing this one."

Mia's mouth popped open. Was she that obvious? "I don't want it if anyone else wants it."

"No one else wants it," Adelaide said, putting it into her hand. "Enjoy!"

"Thank you." She took in a gulp. It was sweet, but not too sweet, and so, so cold. It gave her an instant brain freeze and loosened the knot in her throat.

"Forgive me if I'm wrong," Adelaide said slowly, "but it sounds to me that having a career in film is what your *mom* wants for you. What do *you* want for you?"

Mia pulled on the straw and it honked against the plastic. Normally that would've made her laugh. "I don't know, but she's right. Most women my age would die to get a chance like this. If I don't take advantage of it..." Her voice trailed off. She was just repeating her mom's talking points, the ones that kept her up at night.

"You don't have to do any of it, Mia," Adelaide put a hand on her shoulder. "I'm sure your mom means well. She wants what's best for you. Even still, she may not know what's best for you, and that is what's *so* hard for us moms." She laughed. "Trust me. She's trying, but you have to be the one to decide what you want."

Mia nodded. "Yeah."

"Do you know the poet, Mary Oliver?"

She shook her head.

"She's quite famous, and she had a beautiful poem about what you do with your one wild and precious life. Check it out later."

A grin spread across Mia's face. "Sheila told me you were a professor, but I didn't expect you to assign me homework."

Adelaide laughed. "I taught English as a second language. I'm not exactly a scholar."

"You sound like one to me."

Adelaide's phone rang and she answered. "Oh, okay. Thanks, Joey. We'll head back soon."

Mia's heart sank. It was already time to go back.

"I'm so sorry," Mia said with a groan. "I wasted your time."

Adelaide *tsk*ed. "Don't you dare be sorry. I'm glad we were here. Really glad."

"Maybe I can help with something else? I could go back to Lawrence's neighborhood and see if anyone knows the mystery guys who went door-to-door."

"You don't have to do that," Adelaide said.

"Please," Mia said, dropping her half-empty smoothie into the cup holder. "I need to feel useful, and I could really use a distraction."

Adelaide stared at her. "Are you sure? Getting involved with one of my mom's schemes can be...all-encompassing."

Mia took a deep breath and smiled. "All-encompassing sounds perfect right now."

"Only if it doesn't cause trouble for you."

She popped her sunglasses on and put the car into reverse. "No trouble at all. It'll be nice to get out of my head." Mia forced a smile. "Thanks, Adelaide."

Nine

On the flight back, Addy insisted Rick take the front seat again. It was not an entirely selfless act on her part, but he seemed engaged enough, talking to Joey.

In the back, she was free to dig through Flex Knock's website. She couldn't find any other phone numbers, or even an email to contact someone at the company. She had to fill out the "contact us" form on the website. She added her phone number at the bottom and hit send.

When she searched the address, it showed a run-down strip mall. Was there really an office there? Or was this whole thing a scam? If it was all a scam, maybe Lawrence hadn't really lost his house...

"Sorry I rushed you," Joey said, crackling into Addy's headset. "I can probably bring you out again in a few days. It's just been so busy recently with Lottie's pending arrival."

"I understand," Addy said. "Please don't worry about it. If I need to, I can take the ferry."

"Hopefully you don't get stranded," Joey said. "I really hope they figure something out with the ferries."

"Me too," she said, and she meant it. Though she could think of worse things than being stuck on a beautiful island.

They landed, Russell's dock floating on the glittering water in the distance. After Joey shut off the plane, Addy thanked him for his help, then started up the hill to Patty's cottage. Rick followed an arm's length behind.

"I hope you're not sick of being my bodyguard yet," she said, turning to smile at him.

He shook his head. "Not at all."

"You even got to see some action today."

He nodded. "Yeah."

"You're very strong," Addy said. She stopped walking. "I mean, it was impressive how you picked those guys up."

He stopped, a half-smile pulling at his lips, the dimple flashing ever so briefly. "You were pretty impressive, removing that reporter."

She scoffed. "Some reporter. I looked it up while we were on the plane. There is no Bellingham Star."

"Huh. How about that." He narrowed his eyes. "You're very impressive, too. An investigative reporter yourself."

She let out a laugh. "Yeah, yeah."

Addy kept walking. The door to Patty's cottage was unlocked, as usual. She pushed it open and walked into the cinnamon-filled air.

Eliza must be perfecting a recipe.

She followed the scent to the kitchen. There was no cake. Only Sheila.

"How'd it go?" Sheila asked, setting down the water kettle.

"It was okay. Confusing." Addy took a seat and watched Rick cross through the kitchen and stand by the back door.

He was always on alert. It must be exhausting. Bad for the nerves.

"Actually, wait," Addy said. "What do you know about Mia and this movie she did?"

Sheila shrugged. "Not much. She won't talk to Russell about it, and he wants to let her do her own thing."

"Is it her thing?" Addy asked. "Or her mom's thing?"

Sheila puffed out her lips. "Hard to say." She looked at Rick. "Can I get you something to drink?"

He shook his head and held up the cardboard coffee cup from Bellingham. He'd opted for the so-called oat milk latte. "I'm all set."

"Let me give you some money for the drinks," Addy said, reaching for her purse.

He put up a hand. "It all goes on the company card. Don't worry about it. I'm happy when I get to buy something on their dime."

She studied his face, trying to figure out if that was the truth or if he was trying to be gracious. He had no tells.

Sheila plopped down next to her. "What's Lawrence like? Is he awful?"

Addy shut her eyes. "No. That's the worst part. He's the most lovely man. He says he misses Mom and wants to win her back."

Sheila groaned. "She got another one, eh?"

"I looked through all the paperwork. It was a sale-leaseback like you suspected. They gave him a bit of money and within months, they'd tripled his rent."

"Typical." Sheila shook her head. "I can't believe these companies get away with this stuff."

"We didn't have time to go to the company headquarters," Addy said. "I wish Mom knew what she'd signed."

"If she did business with the actual company, we might have a chance of getting the money back," Sheila said. "But if she didn't..."

"I know." Total disaster. Addy, the spinster sister, would live out the rest of her days catering to her mother's whims. "I'm not going to think about that yet."

Patty breezed into the kitchen and grabbed an apron. "Oh good! You're back!"

"Missed me?" Addy said with a smile.

Maybe if she was good, Patty would adopt her, too. She could be a stepdaughter-in-law or something.

"I was just at the tea shop," Patty said, pulling the apron over her head, "and I ran into your date."

"My date?" Addy glanced at Sheila. "What date?"

"I set up a date for you next week," Patty said, opening a cupboard and pulling out a muffin tin. "He's a *very* handsome man and has a small farm on the west side of the island."

"A farmer," Sheila said, a smile dancing on her lips. "I like that for you."

"I appreciate it, Patty, but I'm not really looking for a date."

"Of course you are! Your ex-husband moved on. Why shouldn't you?"

"It's not about that. I'm busy dealing with my mom, and I've been working on some translations, too."

Sheila's eyes brightened. "What translations?"

A grin broke across Addy's face. "That client who wanted me to translate those articles into Italian? Now he wants me to translate some Italian short stories into English."

"Get out of here!" Sheila slapped her hand on the table. "Congratulations!"

Patty put a hand on her hip. "Is this a new business you're starting?"

Addy nodded. "I've always wanted to work as a translator, but I never had the time when I was working at the university, so I'm giving it a shot. I figure, what have I got to lose?"

"That's exactly what I think about your date." Patty wagged a finger at her, then dropped a paper onto Addy's lap. "This is it. Seven sharp. You're going to love it."

Before Addy could protest, Patty brushed past Rick and out the back door.

Addy stared at the paper. *The Spotted Duck, 7PM, Corey F.*

"Did I just get match-made?" Addy asked.

Sheila erupted into laughter. "I think you did."

Her phone rang. It was her mom. *Again.*

Addy sighed. If this was part of getting adopted by Patty, she'd do it. Plus, her daughter Riley kept encouraging her to put herself out there. What could go wrong?

Ten

The days on the island repeated, sunrises and sunsets over the steady sea. Rick kept close watch on Adelaide, and she spent much of her attention tending to her mother's complaints.

"I'm only going to see her once a day," Adelaide explained. "There have to be rules. I have to be firm, like with a toddler, or she'll walk all over me."

Rick nodded. He knew what it was like to love someone who was exhausting. "That's smart."

Adelaide laughed. "There's nothing smart about it, but it's the best I can do."

They whiled away their afternoons in the tea shop. Adelaide sat at a table, her laptop perched in front of her, a pot of tea within reach. She worked on her translations and Rick sat a few seats away, watching her along with the comings and goings to the little shop. He allowed himself to read as long as it was quiet, never losing sight of the doors.

Though he normally declined tea, Eliza still brought him treats – cakes, cupcakes, cookies. Things she was perfecting. "Free of charge," she'd say, "except the cost of your feedback."

He never had any feedback. Everything was delicious. He wasn't terribly interested in cakes, but her recipes were interesting enough.

Sometimes they sat outside, the seagulls calling above them. He still read, but made sure he was aware of their surroundings. In this case, that meant staring out at the water, watching the birds swoop in, tracking Joey as he took off and landed, took off and landed.

The rhythm and routine should have made it easy for him to sleep. Every night, he thought he might have a chance at some peace.

It was a nice thought. He lay in bed, staring up at the ceiling fan spinning in the shadows. It could get chilly at night, but he didn't close the window. The air was unbelievably clean and fresh. The little sleep he got was often after taking deep breath after deep breath. One night, he swore he heard the blows of a passing pod of orcas.

The only change to their pattern was Friday, when Adelaide had to get ready for her blind date.

"I don't think you need to come to this," she said, standing in front of the mirror and dabbing on mascara.

"This is exactly the sort of thing I need to come to. What if he's a plant?"

Adelaide snorted a laugh. "You think the people who threatened my ex-husband sent a man here to trick Patty and take me on a blind date?"

He shrugged. "You never know."

"As if anyone could trick Patty," she mumbled.

He was inclined to agree with her, but said nothing.

"What's the worst he can do?" She turned to him. "Break my heart?"

Rick laughed. "Regardless, I'm coming."

"I don't know how to explain having a bodyguard." Adelaide said. "'Say hello to my bodyguard, Mr. Bond. No sudden movements.'" She snorted and shook her head.

"I know you want to impress the guy so maybe..." Rick said.

Her jaw dropped. "Are you mocking me?"

He couldn't keep the smile off his face. "No, I'm not mocking you. I can tell you're excited."

"I'm not *excited*," she hissed. "I'm trying to make a sincere effort." She stopped and let out a sigh. "This is all new to me, Rick. I have no idea what I'm doing, but I'm trying to be open to new experiences."

"I'm not criticizing you."

"*I'm* criticizing me," Adelaide said. "In my defense, it's really strange to go from thinking you're happily married to being thrust back out in the cold."

"It is."

"Have you ever been married?" she asked. "Er...are you married?"

Rick cleared his throat. "No."

"Sorry," she said quickly. "I know you don't like to talk about yourself."

"It's not that I don't like to talk about myself," he said. "It's not relevant."

She paused, her hand hanging in the air, clutching a puffy makeup brush. "Of course you're relevant, Rick. You're our fourth roommate."

He laughed. "That's what you can tell your date, then. You brought your roommate along in case things get out of hand."

She turned back to the mirror. "I'm sure that will go over great. I'll seem like a totally sane person."

"You don't have to worry about it," he continued. "I'll go in and grab a table by myself. No one will even know I'm there."

"I wouldn't be so sure." She nudged him with her elbow. "Maybe Patty's got someone lined up for you, too."

He rolled his eyes. "You're getting loony."

She exploded into laughter, hunching over the bathroom sink. When she straightened, streaks of black makeup clumped under her eyelashes. She wiped them away. "I know!"

Rick stepped back. She needed space. She was clearly excited about this date, whether she wanted to admit it or not, and he didn't want to ruin the fun. This date was the first thing Adelaide had done for herself. She was forever at other people's service.

Rick could relate.

He drove them both to the restaurant in Friday Harbor and parked on the street.

"Maybe I should cancel," she said, peering through the window.

The restaurant's sign glowed red in the night, lighting up her face. She looked nice, with the fixed makeup and her hair curled in a new way. It was a waste to run away now.

"I'll walk in behind you and act like I've never seen you before," he said. "It'll be fine."

"You don't have to do that." She shook her head. "I can explain what's going on."

He held up a hand. "Believe me, this will be fine. I prefer hiding in the shadows. You can tell him about me later – if you deem him worthy of knowing about your life."

"Deem him worthy." She repeated slowly. "How do I decide that?"

"That's all of life, isn't it? Deciding who can be trusted, who *should* be trusted with details of your inner life."

"Is that why you don't tell me anything about yourself?" she asked. "Am I unworthy?"

"Exactly, yes. You're unworthy."

He popped his door open. Adelaide erupted into another bout of manic laughter, doubling over as she tried to open her door.

Rick jogged to her side of the car and opened it. "Mrs. Ashbourne? This way. They're expecting you."

She stepped out of the car. "I don't think I can do this, Rick."

"Of course you can. You're already doing it." He nodded toward the restaurant. "You're halfway there."

She sighed and walked to the door.

Rick trailed behind, walking in a few moments later. The restaurant was poorly lit, the small tables scattered like marbles. Warm candles glowed on each one.

Straight ahead was a bar. The bottles were illuminated by a purple glow. A man spotted Adelaide and stood up.

She walked over to him as Rick took a seat at the bar.

"Adelaide?" The man said.

"Hi, Corey?"

She went in for a hug, he went in for the handshake. They danced for a moment before landing on a side hug.

Painful.

Rick sat at the end of the bar. He picked up a menu and pretended to study it.

"It's so nice to meet you," he said. "Patty told me you're her... granddaughter?"

"No, not her granddaughter," Adelaide said with a laugh. "I'm her ex-daughter-in-law's sister..." She paused. "Which is more confusing than it needs to be."

"Ha, yeah."

She took a seat, and he sat next to her.

"I'm starting to wonder if Patty misrepresented me."

He took a sip of water. "Misrepresented?"

Rick looked up. The guy's mouth was open, his eyes wide. Deer in the headlights.

"I'm sure she was coming from a good place," Adelaide said. "But I am in no way young enough to be her granddaughter."

The guy laughed. "Oh, right."

"I don't mean to be rude," Adelaide continued, "but how old are you?"

"Twenty-nine."

Rick couldn't stop himself from staring now. Yeah, the guy looked young. He hadn't been sure before, but he was young. Not that Adelaide was old, but she wasn't twenty-nine.

She laughed and shook her head. "Good old Patty."

"Was that the wrong answer?" the guy laughed.

She shook her head. "No, no. It's just – well, I'm forty-eight. I'm old enough to be..."

"My mother!" he said with a laugh.

Adelaide pulled back. "I wouldn't go that far."

Oh man. Regardless of age, this guy wasn't mature enough to be talking to Adelaide. Rick took off his coat. It was getting hot in here with all the secondhand embarrassment.

Maybe he'd order a root beer float. Anything to distract himself from this.

Adelaide went on. "The truth is, it would be more appropriate for you to take my daughter out to dinner than to take me out to dinner. It was nice meeting you, but we don't have to do this."

Corey placed one foot on the ground, as though he was ready to stand. Ready to flee. "I'd hate to put you out."

That was enough. Adelaide didn't need to deal with this kid. Rick stood from his barstool and closed the distance between them. "Adelaide, hi."

"Hi." A slow smile spread across her face, her eyes darting between them. "How are you?"

"So funny running into you here," Rick said. "Are you headed to dinner?"

She looked at her date. "I..."

"I don't mean to barge in," Rick said. He offered a handshake. "Nice to meet you."

Corey stuck out his hand. "Likewise." The guy had a firm handshake. He wasn't handling this super gracefully, but it could've been worse.

Correction – it could still get worse. Best to get the kid out of here.

Adelaide turned to Corey. "Listen, you're very polite, but don't worry about me. You should go off and do young people things. It was nice meeting you."

He shot to his feet. "It was nice meeting you too! Tell Patty I say hi!"

He disappeared and Rick turned to Adelaide. She'd collapsed on the shiny tabletop, her face in her arms.

"There were a lot of ways I thought this could've gone wrong," she said, her voice muffled, "but that wasn't one I'd expected."

"Worry is rarely an effective means by which to mold the future," Rick said.

Her head popped up, hair flipped over her one eye. "Did you come up with that yourself?"

He shrugged. "I'm not sure. Maybe I read it in a book."

She dragged herself to her feet. "Well, my embarrassment is complete. Let's go back to the house and pretend this never happened."

"Aren't we going to eat?" Rick asked. "I'm hungry."

"It's bad enough you had to witness that," Adelaide said, smoothing her hair. "I'm not going to hold you hostage for dinner, blathering on about myself."

"You know," he said slowly, "I could stand to chat, too. Your status changed."

"My status?"

"You've been deemed –"

"Don't say worthy," she said, shaking her head. "I can't bear it, Rick. I just can't."

"Trustworthy," he said.

"Why? Because you've seen me at my lowest? Called old by a blind date? Being accused of being said date's mother?"

He laughed. "I think he was bad at math."

She rolled her eyes. "Not technically, no. If I were eighteen and I –"

Rick cut her off. "I'm trying to tell you my secrets, Adelaide, and all you can do is talk about technicalities."

A smile spread across her face. "We'd better hurry up and get a table before you change your mind."

Eleven

The place was nearly empty, so the hostess told them to pick a table. Addy chose one near the window. A single, yellow LED lamp shaped like a candle glowed in the center, casting its warm glow with a calming, artificial flicker.

They sat and Addy picked up a menu. The appetizers looked good. So did the salads, and the gnocchi.

If she had to be humiliated, she at least deserved gnocchi.

"I joined the army right after high school," Rick said, setting his menu down.

Addy looked up at him. He was getting right to business. "When was that?"

"2002."

The math flipped through her mind. He was forty. Only eight years younger than her.

Ha. *Only*.

"Wait. 2002?" Her hand darted to her mouth.

He nodded. "Yup. A few months after enlisting, I deployed to Iraq."

"You were a kid." She shook her head. "That must have been hard."

He sucked in a breath, scrubbing the stubble on his chin with his hand. "I went in as a bright eyed, eighteen-year-old boy and after thirteen months there..." He shook his head. "I wasn't that boy anymore."

"My dad served in Vietnam," Addy said. "He didn't like to talk about it. He told me it was very boring, except when it wasn't."

Rick smiled, creasing at the corner of his eyes. "That's accurate. It's waiting around until all hell breaks loose." He paused. "Excuse my language. War is the worst thing on earth."

"You're excused." She'd heard far worse from her dad's friends. "I am not one to judge a person who served our country."

He leaned in, resting his elbows on the table and his head on his hands. "You know, I got lucky. After I was discharged, my uncle made me talk to someone. He was a shrink for the VA and he refused to let me hide away."

"Like a therapist?" Something that hadn't been available to her dad. He'd only had his friends and the sea. He did okay, but Addy always worried about him.

"Yeah. A therapist. I'm not ashamed to admit it. I needed to sort out what happened. Set my head straight. Not that I'll ever fully understand. War can't be understood, because it doesn't make sense. That's that hard thing to understand." He sighed. "Anyway, I'm not saying I'm perfect, but it helped. I had too many friends who came back from deployment but couldn't put themselves together again. There were too many broken pieces. Too much..." His voice trailed off.

Her mouth was gaping. Rick didn't seem like someone who could be broken into pieces. He was solid as stone.

Still, the world managed to crack him. It made it hard to not stand up and hug him.

He cleared his throat. "Too much destruction. I've always wanted to start a post-bootcamp or something. For the guys coming home. Like a debrief of everything they'd witnessed. Everything they'd done."

The light illuminated a golden hue in his caramel eyes. Addy's chest froze, a breath caught in her throat

"After that, I was a paramedic," he continued, "but I burned out after a few years."

"That's a stressful job."

He nodded. "The stress was what I liked about it. High stakes. I wanted to see if I could still react when it mattered." He laughed. "Turns out I could, though most of it was boring, too. But when I needed to, I could keep my cool, and that was important to prove to myself."

"You are very good at keeping your cool," Addy said. "Unlike me before a blind date."

Rick grinned. "That was very..."

"Unhinged? Yes, I know." Addy nodded, straightening a cloth napkin in her lap. "I am the queen of losing my cool."

He tilted his head down, peering at her. "I was going to say endearing."

"Ha, right." She pulled her menu in front of her face. Hopefully she'd moved quickly enough to block the blush blooming on her cheeks.

The waitress stopped by. Addy ordered the gnocchi. Rick ordered the grilled chicken margherita.

Once their orders were in, Rick spoke again. "I used the GI Bill to go to school."

She leaned in. "What did you study?"

"Philosophy and history. Double major."

Addy dropped her hand to the table. "Get out! Philosophy?"

"I guess I was still trying to understand the world." He shook his head. "I haven't figured it out yet."

Addy shrugged. "At least you're trying."

He kept talking, picking up momentum. "When I was in college, I did some work as a bouncer and got a few jobs with private security companies. I did a master's in security studies and got pulled into the corporate security world."

He hadn't said this many words to her perhaps the entire time they'd known each other. Maybe he'd been waiting for someone to talk to. Big, tough Rick was finally feeling comfortable enough to talk to old, unthreatening Adelaide.

Being herself had its perks. Whenever she used to have to puff herself up to confront one of Riley's teachers at school, Shane used to laugh and say she was as threatening as a church mouse.

Yet even a church mouse had its place in the world, and right now it was at this table, listening to the past of a fascinating man who didn't often find people worth talking to.

The joke was on Shane.

Addy couldn't keep the smile off her face. "Let me guess. You hated it."

He laughed. "Yeah, I sort of did. It was too stable." He raised his arm, his muscles outlined in shadows, and scratched the back of his neck. "Kidding, but I was bored to tears."

"And you made too much money."

He leaned in. "How did you know that? Did you have me checked out?"

"Yes. Full background check. I know everything." She grinned. "Just kidding. It was a guess."

Rick sat back and crossed his arms over his chest. "I made a lot. More than I needed. I didn't want it."

"So you decided to come to San Juan Island for a vacation?"

Rick looked down, quiet for a moment.

Oh no. She'd crossed a line.

He looked up, waving a hand. "Nah, I wouldn't put it that way. A friend of mine asked for a favor. I was looking for a change, and here I am."

If she'd touched on something she wasn't supposed to, he didn't give any hints about it for the rest of the meal.

Their food arrived and they feasted, laughing and talking over one another. By the end, she was stuffed, the sting of her blind date rejection long gone.

Addy sat back, pushing her plate away. "I have to say, getting into your circle of trust was worth the wait."

He smiled a half smile, that dimple lighting up. "Yeah?"

"Yeah."

"What about you? I've talked your ear off."

She rolled her eyes. "You know about me. Divorced. One daughter, Riley, the light of my life. Crazy mother. Angry older sister..."

He laughed. "You're a professor?"

"I was. English as a second language. I studied German and Italian in college and was close to mastering Spanish as well. While you were trying to understand the world, I was a foolish young girl with dreams of living in Italy."

"I love Italy. I'm sure there's a lot about life the Italians could teach me. Did you ever get to live there?"

"Just one year, studying abroad in college. It was lovely. Then I met my husband and we settled in Canada. He didn't like to travel, so –"

"What a chump. Is that why you divorced him?"

A laugh burst out of her. "We were married for nineteen years and no. We'd just grown apart. After the divorce, I was laid off from the university. I was...pretty lost, to be honest. Sheila convinced me to come to the island."

"Lost." He bowed his head. "Essentially, we're in the same spot in life."

She scrunched her forehead. "What do you mean?"

"Lost. Drifting at sea."

He didn't seem lost to her, but Addy wasn't going to invalidate his reality. Not when he'd opened up like that. "I guess you could look at it that way. Except you're much younger than I am."

He lifted a shoulder. "Nah. What's a couple of years between friends?"

"Friends." She grinned. "I like that for us."

He smiled. "Me too."

Twelve

S he was far too easy to talk to. Rick hadn't meant to tell her all those things. Maybe one or two events from his past, but *everything* about himself?

Yikes.

He normally didn't get this far. People forced him to stop talking when they asked rude questions. "How many people have you shot?" or "What's the worst thing you saw on the ambulance?"

They said it with a smile, too, like they were waiting to hear an exciting story, not one about the worst day of his life.

There was none of that from Adelaide. It was like talking to someone who'd known him all his life.

On the drive home, she was quiet. He thought she might be waiting for him to spill more secrets. He kept his mouth shut.

When they were almost at the house, she turned to him and said, "Thanks for the pity dinner."

He pulled into the driveway, shaking his head.

"There was no pity," he said, stopping at the house. "I was hungry, and I needed to get more use out of that company card."

"Uh huh."

"We were two ships passing in the night," he continued. "Two ships adrift in the same restaurant –"

Her uproarious laughter cut him off. He smiled to himself and shut off the engine. The night fell silent, save for the wind sweeping leaves across the ground.

Adelaide popped her door open. "I appreciate our," she paused, "relation*ship*."

He groaned. "You're terrible."

She laughed again, jumping from the car and shutting the door.

Rick didn't mean it, of course. Her spirit was back, as strong as before. He stepped out of the car, hiding his smile. The house looked different in the moonlight. Softer, somehow, the warm glow from the windows inviting them in.

Adelaide pushed the door open—it was unlocked, as always—and turned to look at him. Light flooded around her, illumining the gentle smile on her face.

His heart leapt. Another glimpse into a different life. Adelaide looking back at him, waiting for him. A place called home. A safe place.

"Everything okay?" she asked.

Snap back to reality. "Yeah, sorry."

He followed her inside. The kitchen was empty. No sign of Sheila.

He liked Sheila well enough, but he didn't want her to hear about Adelaide's night yet. For this moment, it was between her and Rick. A small secret he got to keep.

She went upstairs and retired to her room. He said his goodnights, then went back to his room and opened the window. After a shower, he laid down on the bed, a towel still wrapped around his waist.

The ocean was calm tonight, barely any sound at all. The wind whistled in the window, the cold air a stark contrast to the warmth of the bed.

Rick's eyes drifted shut, and his arms and legs sank into the bed, anchoring him into place. His breaths grew long and deep.

The shrill pangs of his alarm shocked him awake. Rick sat up, his heart thundering in his chest.

He rarely made it to his alarm, always waking early and restless from whatever broken sleep he'd claimed.

He got dressed quickly and rushed to Addy's door. Inside, she sang a tune.

"Are you okay in there?" he called out.

"Yes, just getting ready! I have good news."

He shouldn't have slept so deeply. What if something had happened? He hadn't woken all night. Hadn't heard anything.

Sweat dotted his forehead. He wiped it away with the back of his hand.

He returned to his room to brush his teeth and splash cold water on his face. When Addy's door opened, he was waiting to walk her down the stairs.

"Mia sent me a message," Addy said, showing him her phone. "She talked to some people in Lawrence's neighborhood, and one had doorbell footage of the guys who were going door-to-door."

"That's interesting."

"Do you have access to some sort of database? Maybe we can put their pictures in and identify these guys?"

Rick smiled. "No, I don't have access to a facial recognition database, and I wish no one did."

She sighed. "Here I thought you were high tech." She pulled a pan from the cupboard and set it on the stove. "Egg sandwich?"

It wasn't her responsibility to feed him. But those sandwiches were so good...

"If it's not a bother."

"Not at all," she said, turning to the fridge. "One of the neighbors gave Mia a business card. It has a different address than the one on the website. Maybe we should check it out?"

It was a terrible idea. This company was shady in some way, and these guys were just the start of it. They should leave it alone and help Marilyn find a new place to live. Maybe talk to a social worker and find her senior assistance.

Adelaide stopped, a carton of eggs in her hand, and peered up at him.

Who was he to squash the hope in her eyes? "Whatever you think is best."

"I knew I liked you," she said with a wag of her finger.

She turned, flicking water into the pan. Little beads of liquid jumped into place, bouncing against the edges. Adelaide threw in a glob of butter. She cracked one egg, then a second.

It was rude to stare. Rick picked up the coffee pot and turned away. The smell of the coffee beans helped him focus.

Still – why had his heart jumped when she said that?

Thirteen

The view from the ferry window was breathtaking, spanning the entirety of their booth, showing off the passing bluffs and impenetrable tree lines of the passing islands.

Rick sat across from her, reading, always reading, this time a bent paperback.

Addy peered up, tracing the lines of his face. She'd finally gotten to see behind that scowl. War, philosophy, corporate life. There was even more to him than she'd suspected.

She must've really embarrassed herself at dinner. What other reason could there be for Rick's sudden change in personality? Confessing his secrets, as he put it.

At the same time, Addy refused to feel embarrassed. She was too old for that. All things considered, the awkwardness of the blind date had been Patty's fault, and Addy had handled it well. She let the poor guy off the hook and still had a nice evening, thanks to Rick.

It was a kindness on his part – talking about his vulnerabilities after getting an open view of hers. Addy had that effect on people. She could be so hapless, so chaotic, that people didn't feel self-conscious about spilling their secrets to her. *Addy won't judge me,* they think. *She's a mess!*

Addy didn't mind. It was who she was, and she wouldn't apologize for it. The first time she'd truly doubted herself was after the divorce, but that was to be expected. The one person who had always thought the world of her had suddenly changed his mind.

She now knew it had more to do with him than it did with her, but of course it still hurt. Shane had gone through a cliché midlife crisis, refusing to let anyone help him. All the issues he'd built up during his life – many going back to his childhood – had crashed over him like a tsunami and washed their shared life away.

Shane's new girlfriend fit the textbook midlife crisis case, too: sixteen years his junior, a fan of posting pictures of the two of them driving in his new red convertible.

What could Addy do but laugh?

It was like the ground had opened after the divorce, a sinkhole no one knew was there. Maybe she'd felt rumblings, but it was too ridiculous to believe.

She'd doubted herself in every way afterward, and though she'd made a lot of progress, she was still picking up the pieces. Her greatest fear, tucked into that wine bottle in Russell's house, lurked behind every thought. *Am I worthy of love? Are my best years behind me, or was I never all that great to begin with?*

Maybe she was nothing more than chaos and happenstance. She couldn't keep her marriage from imploding, yet she thought she could track down her mom's stolen money?

"I hope this isn't too forward," Rick said, setting the book down.

Addy snapped her head back toward him. "Oh?"

He stared at her with those penetrating eyes. "Has your mom always been like this?"

She bit her lip to stop the smile creeping across her face. "What do you mean?"

He hesitated, "Well –"

A laugh sprung out of her chest. It was too hard to keep a straight face. "I'm messing with you. Yes. Always has been, always will be." She shook her head. "Sheila and I still talk to Mom, but my youngest sister, Kara, cut off contact."

"You're a middle child?" He smiled. "That explains so much."

"Excuse you, now you *are* being too forward," she said, slapping a hand on the table between them.

"No, it's just –" He looked down at his hands, shaking his head. "You're a capable middle child, that's all."

"Right." She cracked a smile. "Mom left us when we were little. I was seven when she just disappeared. Left our dad to take care of us."

"When did she come back?"

"I don't remember exactly. She popped back in, but before long, she took off again. She always had an excuse. There was always an adventure, someone she'd met, some secret she'd found. Something she was chasing." Addy shook her head. "I stopped trying to understand it a long time ago."

"It's a credit to you that you haven't cut her out of your life entirely."

Addy sighed. "I thought about it. I respect Kara for her choice. The truth is, it's a lot of work to cut a family member out of your life. Maybe just as much as keeping them in." She realized she was biting her lip again. "In the end, I decided I wanted to keep the relationship for myself. Though, right now, as four texts just popped up from her, I'm questioning it."

He laughed. "I understand what it's like. You can still love someone even if they're troubled."

"Troubled..." Addy looked up. The sky was a rich, infinite blue. If she squinted, it flowed right into the sea. "I don't know if *troubled* is the right word for her. I'm sure there are a lot of clinical terms for it nowadays."

"I can think of a few."

She grinned. "It's not worth going into it. I've learned to only give her as much as I can and no more. I can't let myself be guilted by her."

"Right. You aren't responsible for her choices," he said slowly. "It's a wise theory, but can be hard in practice."

She looked at him. He was resting his face on his hands, his eyes hard, staring down at the table.

"Are you okay, Rick?" she asked.

His eyes darted up. "Yeah, of course, Adelaide."

She cocked her head to the side. "When are you gonna start calling me Addy?"

He shrugged. "Is it professional to call you Addy?"

"I thought we were friends," she said.

He smiled, and her pulse quickened at the appearance of that dimple.

"We are." He sat back, looking her square in the eyes. "Addy."

She smiled, looking back to the sea. "Good."

An announcement for passengers to return to their cars came over the loudspeaker. Addy stood first and Rick followed. They walked down the steps to the level with their car. Rick jogged ahead to get the door for her.

"You don't have to do that," she said. "I appreciate it, but it's not your job."

"I don't get to do much else because you're so good at defending yourself," he said. "Consider it a security feature."

Security feature. She laughed as he shut the door.

He wasn't wrong. Just him being there made her feel more secure. She never would've done something like this before – chasing leads, looking for scammers.

She couldn't live doubting herself. Her best days couldn't be behind her. Rick had reinvented himself half a dozen times. Couldn't she manage just once?

They drove off the ferry and into Anacortes, winding along the picturesque houses, dashes of sea and mountains in the distance.

It was nearly an hour's drive to Bellingham. Addy had a Kishi Bashi album queued up that suited the mood, but when she asked Rick what he wanted to listen to, he rattled off facts about an audiobook he had called *Mindhunter: Inside the FBI's Elite Serial Crime Unit*.

"It's by John Douglas, an old FBI guy," Rick said as he pulled up chapter five. "It's a crazy story of how he and his unit at the FBI started looking into the psychology behind serial killers. Interviewing them."

Addy raised her eyebrows. "Not the most soothing listening for this trip."

Rick laughed. "I don't think we're up against serial killers. Probably just common criminals, but it's important to understand how they think. He always stresses that criminals don't think like regular people."

He was probably right, but she didn't like thinking like a criminal. The guys she was looking for, however, very well could be.

Mia had sent pictures of the two men who had gone door-to-door, along with a picture of their calling card. There were no names, but an address was listed.

Addy confirmed with her mom that those were the men she'd talked to when she'd signed paperwork and handed over a bag of money. She didn't recall their names, either. Anonymity seemed important at this company.

It would've scared the old Addy off, but not the new Addy. She was going to figure this out if it was the last thing she did.

They arrived at the address and pulled into a slim parking lot for a strip mall. Rick navigated around a runaway shopping cart in the middle of the driving lane, then cringed as the car plunged into a pothole.

"This place looks nice," he said evenly, pulling into a parking spot. The paint was faded and chipped.

Addy groaned. "It's even worse than the motel."

"I wish Lawrence was here."

She shot him a look. There was a half-smile on his lips. "Don't you wish this horrible place on sweet old Lawrence."

Rick grinned, popping open his door. There were four businesses in the strip mall, plus a space that said **FOR RENT**, with a phone number scrawled in black marker.

The address Mia had given them pointed to the space wedged between a nail salon and a place called uHealth Labs. They got out of the car and walked toward the building. The air smelled of acetone and fried food.

Two doors stood in front of them; one unmarked, and one with a metal box hanging from it that read **DO NOT LEAVE BLOOD SAMPLES OVERNIGHT.**

"Ew," Addy whispered.

Rick shrugged, pulling the other door open.

It was dark inside. Her eyes struggled to adjust, scanning the wood paneling walls and the single cubicle divider, a desk on either side.

A man sat behind one of the desks, watching them as they walked closer. His round belly touched the tabletop, his greased combover reflecting the fluorescent lighting.

"Can I help you?" he asked.

"Yes," Addy said slowly. "I'm here to talk to someone from Flex Knock."

He nodded, flipping a folder closed. "This about a house?"

"It is."

"Have a seat." He gestured, his hands like paddles, the thick, meaty fingers strangled by a flurry of gold rings.

Two chairs sat in front of the desk. Rick motioned for her to sit first.

"I'm so very sorry that you are having trouble with your house," he said flatly, as though reading each word from a giant teleprompter. "We are here to help."

"I was actually hoping to talk to the guys I talked to before," Addy said. She pulled out her phone, holding up a grainy shot of the two men. "I don't remember their names."

"Don't worry about them." He waved a paddle. "I can help you."

"I'd prefer to talk to them," Addy said. "My mom signed a contract with them. Her name is Marilyn Osborne."

He put his hands together. "They do something to you?"

Addy shot a look at Rick. His eyes were fixed on the man.

"Do something? Like what?" she asked.

"You tell me, lady. You're coming in here making demands, talking about a contract. We don't have any contracts with Marilyn Osborne."

"How can you know that without looking it up?" She cleared her throat. "These guys gave me a card with this address. My mom paid in cash."

"I'll tell you what you need to know," he said. "Do you want to work with us or not?"

"Not." Rick stood. "I think it's time to go."

The guy looked at the folder on his desk, flipping it open. "Yeah, good. Take your boyfriend with you."

Addy felt herself being propelled toward the door. Rick had his hand on her arm.

"I'm not ready to go," she whispered.

"He's ready for us to go," he said.

The door opened. Addy looked up – Rick's arm was above her, all bulging muscle and force.

How was she going to fight that?

"Fine," she said, "but this isn't over."

"Don't let the door hit ya!" the man behind the desk yelled.

Addy rolled her eyes. This was far from over.

Fourteen

There was nothing for them in that rat nest. That guy had no interest in talking unless he could steal a house from them. Rick was done with it.

They got back in the car and Addy slammed her door shut.

Rick spoke first. "I know you're not happy with me."

"I could've gotten him to talk!" she said, turning to him. "Or if we'd stayed around long enough, those guys would've shown up."

"You think they would have talked to you? Especially after you told them you're the daughter of the lady they took a bag of money from?" He shook his head. "It wasn't going anywhere. None of those guys will admit to anything. The whole operation looks like a farce."

"Can we at least call the police? Report that they stole her money?"

Rick looked back at the door. The guy who had chased them out stood at the window, his belly pressed against the glass.

He started the car and pulled out of the parking spot. "Maybe. It would help if you'd found the guys' real names, but even then, if you file a police report, what can they do? Question them and see if they admit to it?"

"They need to open an investigation!"

Rick sighed. "This isn't *Law and Order*. The local cops don't have the time to track down leads every time someone gets scammed."

Addy crossed her arms over her chest. "She signed a contract. Maybe we can sue them."

"Maybe." Judging from that office, it didn't look like Flex Knock or its employees, had much to sue *for*. He decided to keep that to himself.

They drove on. The company car was much nicer than what he had at home. Despite potholes and uneven surfaces, it was quiet as a church mouse inside the cabin.

All he could hear was Addy sighing and shifting. She kept her eyes fixed on the window.

"Giving up is not an option," she finally announced. "I may not have figured out what to do with the rest of my life, but I can't live with my mother."

He glanced over at her. "How is *that* an option? What happened to boundaries?"

"She's broke, and I can't afford to house her anywhere else, so that's where this is headed if I can't find her money. I just got laid off and divorced at the same time. It's almost as bad as handing over a bag of money to strangers, so I have to figure this out."

"I'd say your way of losing money is different. Much more time-consuming."

She sighed, a slight smile on her face. "It is."

"Where do you want to go?" He asked. "Back to the neighborhood? Back to the ferry?"

She was staring again. Then she added a quiet, "I don't know."

He drove on. The sky opened in front of them, buildings easing into the background. A large red barn stood in the distance. Rows of apple trees lined the road.

"Want to go apple picking?" he asked, smiling.

"No, thank you."

If they kept driving, they'd end up in Canada. "Listen, how about I look into Flex Knock? I can use my contacts and see if there's anything else useful."

"You said you didn't have contacts." She turned to him now, smiling, her eyes narrowed.

He tilted his head. "I said I didn't have facial recognition technology. I never said I don't have contacts."

She laughed. "Ah, right. Yes, I'd appreciate it."

"Consider it done."

She uncrossed her arms. "Do you want to get something to eat? I'm starving."

"I thought you'd never ask."

He pulled off immediately where an underwhelming sign read **FARM CAFE.**

"I've got a good feeling about this place."

She nodded. "Me too."

After lunch, they went back to Lawrence's neighborhood and sat in the car, watching.

No suspicious salesmen appeared. Rick didn't mind. Addy agreed to listen to his audiobook, but after two hours of hearing about murderers, she was ready to get back home.

They left Bellingham empty handed except for the apple pie Rick had bought for Russell and Sheila.

• • •

It took a week and a half to hear back from his buddy in forensic accounting. Flex Knock was nothing but a shell company. They'd only been in operation for two years, and there was no owner and no real traces of assets. It led to another shell company, then another, before disappearing.

"They'll probably close up shop when they get enough complaints," his buddy told him, "then open under a new name, transferring all the contracts."

"Would she be able to sue them?"

"Unlikely. They'd declare bankruptcy before moving everything over."

"Great. Thanks for checking."

"No problem."

Rick hung up and looked for his charge. Addy sat at the picnic table outside of the tea shop, her computer in front of her, her hair blowing in the wind. She paused for a moment, raising a hand to rub her forehead.

Instinctively, he wanted to look away, as though she might catch him staring.

That was his job, though.

She put her hands back on her keyboard and resumed typing.

He was allowed to look at her, even if she was a beautiful woman. Rick had to remind himself of that.

There was more to Addy than beauty, anyway. She had that in spades – but then there was her laugh, her confidence, the way she walked like she was floating...

She seemed to have little notice of the effect she had on men...or she was too polite to use it to her advantage.

Addy looked up and caught his eye. "Hey."

His heart thudded against his ribs.

"Hey," he said, walking over and taking a seat at the table.

She took a deep breath and closed her eyes. "Beautiful today, isn't it?"

Rick stared at her. "It's beautiful every day."

She laughed. "So it is."

"I've got some bad news," he continued. "My buddy got back to me about Flex Knock."

"Let me guess. He couldn't find anything."

"Sort of. They're a shell company, owned by no one, some LLC registered offshore." He paused. So far, no reaction. "He's pretty good at this, though, and managed to track down the next link, but it was just another offshore LLC."

Addy closed her eyes again. "My mom's money was deposited into an account in the Cayman Islands, wasn't it?"

"Probably."

She shut her laptop and focused her cool gray eyes on him. "You seem like you have more bad news to tell me."

He jerked backward slightly, like she'd snapped her fingers in front of him. "I do?"

"Go ahead, spit it out. I can handle it."

He'd wanted to find the right way to say this, the right amount of information to tell her. It felt like he could tell her anything, but why did she deserve to be burdened with his problems?

"There is one more thing." Rick scratched the back of his neck.

She tilted her head slightly. "Yes?"

"They're going to have to send a guy out here to be my temporary replacement."

Her eyes widened. "Did I do something to offend you?"

"No, of course not. It's nothing like that. I have a personal event I need to attend. It'll be no more than twenty-four hours."

Ask me. Ask what it is. I'll tell you.

"Oh," she said. "Of course. Whatever you need, Rick."

"I hate to do this, but I'll get the guy caught up on everything and make sure you're safe."

"Sure."

He went on. "I have a request. Please don't run off while I'm away. If you're going to look into Flex Knock any more –"

He stopped talking when he saw the smile creeping across her face.

"Uh huh," he said, pointing a finger. "Don't you ever give up?"

"Of course I give up!" she said. "Just not until it's reason-able."

Rick shut his eyes. "Please be reasonable until I get back."

"I will be," she said, nodding. "Pinky swear."

He laughed. "All right, then."

Fifteen

She'd wanted to keep her word to Rick. Addy had intended to stick around the house and catch up on work while he was away. She hadn't planned anything nefarious.

But then she got a call from Mia. What was she supposed to do, ignore an amazing opportunity to talk to the two guys who had hoodwinked her mom?

Time was of the essence. Mia's neighborhood contact reported they were a few streets over, going door to door.

Addy dropped the frying pan in the sink. There was no time for eggs. Her new temporary bodyguard, Phil, had refused her offer anyway, retracting with horror at the word *fried*.

He was younger than Rick by about fifteen years, and had told her with complete sincerity, "I'm sure your cooking is great, but I don't keep ten percent body fat by eating fried foods."

She grabbed a granola bar and her coat. "We're taking a flight!"

"Right behind you," he said.

He didn't stop to grab a coat, instead pausing by the door to steal a look at himself in the mirror before they left.

Addy jogged down to the dock. Joey was waiting, the seaplane tied off.

"Thanks for doing this. I know it's last minute," Addy said as she jumped into the backseat.

"Happy to help!" Joey said.

"Hey man, good to meet you," Phil said, vigorously shaking Joey's hand. "Cool plane."

"Thanks."

Addy looked down, pretending to focus on her seat belt. Was she just too used to Rick, or did Phil lack a certain cynicism, a worldliness one desired in a bodyguard?

It didn't matter.

"I'm hoping we won't take too long," Addy said.

Joey climbed into his seat. "Don't worry about it. I have to pick someone up from Bellingham in two hours anyway."

"That should be plenty of time," Addy said.

They took off. Addy debated filling Phil in on what was happening, but he spent the entire flight asking Joey so many questions that she didn't have a chance.

He wasn't curious about her. That was fine. Better, maybe.

They landed in Bellingham. Addy thanked Joey, then off she went in search of Mia's car. She found it parked on the street.

Mia rolled her window down and stuck her hand out. She jiggled a black canister in her hand. "See that? The strongest pepper spray that's legal in the US."

Addy laughed. "Did Rick tell you to buy that?"

"He had it sent to my house!" she said. "How'd he even know where I live?"

Addy paused. That man had a lot of mysteries around him. "I have no idea. Have you needed to use it?"

"Not yet, but I feel more confident."

Addy stepped to the side. "Mia, this is Phil. He's covering until Rick gets back tomorrow."

"Hi, Phil."

"Take a seat," Addy said, pulling open the car door. "We've got to hurry. I hope they're not gone yet."

"Friends of yours?" Phil asked.

"Not exactly." Addy turned to Mia. "Who is this neighborhood lookout you've been talking to? Do you have spies?"

Mia laughed. "It's this one lady I met by Lawrence's old house. She's lived there for fifty years. She knows *everyone*, and she felt awful about what happened to Lawrence. She and the other neighbors started a neighborhood watch for the salesmen."

"Incredible." Addy shook her head. "You're like a detective."

"It's been great to have something to do. I check in there almost every day. It's been a good distraction." She lowered her voice. "I've been thinking about what you said, too."

"Oh?"

"Yeah. I don't know what I'm going to do yet, but I had never considered anything else. It's really made me think."

Addy smiled. "I'm glad I could be of some use."

They arrived at a neighborhood with streets arranged in an orderly grid. Mia cruised the first street slowly, scanning the houses along the way. "They were last spotted here. I guess they could be inside someone's house…"

She gasped. "There they are! In the blue shirts."

"Are these guys a threat?" Phil asked, leaning forward from the back seat.

"I don't think so," Addy said. "But they stole some money from my mom."

"That's not cool."

Not cool indeed, Phil.

"Do you mind standing behind us and looking intimidating?" Mia asked. "I have a plan."

"That's what I'm here for!" Phil unbuckled his seat belt, a grin on his face.

He looked like a high school kid to Addy. Maybe it was best to leave him in the car…

"Follow my lead," Mia said. "I've been practicing all week."

Addy raised her eyebrows. As much as she wanted to talk to these guys, she hadn't thought of what to say.

That was foolish. Poor planning on her part. At least Mia was on top of it.

"You have my full trust," Addy said, getting out of the car, her heart pounding.

Mia led the way, her head high and her shoulders back. Addy walked next to her, Phil following closely behind.

"Hey there!" Mia shouted. "I've been looking for you two."

They were the blurry picture come to life – young guys, probably Phil's age, though not as baby-faced. The shorter one had a shaved head and a gold hoop at the top of his ear. The other guy had blond hair—almost white—and rounded Muppet eyes.

"Oh yeah?" the shorter one said. A smile crossed his face.

Mia crossed her arms over her chest. "I heard you're getting people good deals for their houses."

Addy looked at her. How had she not noticed Mia was wearing a dress and heels until now? She looked like a model.

Addy looked down at herself. A raincoat and grey hiking pants that swished with every step. She looked like her daughter's old school nurse, the one who'd quit nursing to become a nun.

"We've got the best deals. You live around here?"

"Maybe I do," Mia said.

She smiled and both guys looked at each other, grinning.

A shudder crawled down Addy's back. For the first time, she wished Rick was with them.

She stepped forward. "We're having some trouble with our mortgage payments."

The smile slipped from the short one's face. Nothing like a non-flirty woman to ruin the mood.

"We can help you with that, ma'am," Muppet Eyes said. "How about we go to your house and talk?"

"Hang on." Mia held up a finger. "I need to see some ID first."

Addy had to bite her lip. Mia was bold, yes, but she had a plan.

They both plunged their hands into their pockets and pulled out matching ID cards, blue and white, the Flex Knock logo seared at the top.

Mia leaned in. "Richard Callingford and Kenny Kingpin?" She tilted her head to the side. "These cannot be your real names."

The bald one broke first. "Ha, yeah, we try to keep some anonymity. This can be a tough business."

"I bet." Mia crossed her arms over her chest again. "I don't do business with fake people."

The blond one dug into his pocket and pulled out a wallet, fumbling until he pulled out a driver's license. "Here."

"Sebastian Malone," Mia said, tapping her chin. "And you?"

The bald guy sighed, but he too produced his driver's license. His real name was Julian Tate.

Mia held up the licenses, and Addy managed to silently snap a picture of them.

If she called the police now, maybe they could arrest them on the spot. Maybe they'd admit to stealing the money!

It was too much. Too much tension, too much of creepy men leering at Mia. Addy had enough.

"Do you remember Marilyn?" Addy asked. "Little old lady who lived a few streets over?"

Julian shrugged. "We meet a lot of people."

"She should be pretty memorable," Addy said. "She signed a contract with you and handed over fifty thousand dollars in cash."

Sebastian put his hands up. "Whoa whoa. That is quite an allegation. We don't deal with the money."

Julian shook his head. "We're just the salesmen."

"I need to see the contract she signed," Addy said.

"Ma'am, the old lady probably got confused. I'm pretty sure I'd remember getting a bag of money," Julian said, smirking.

"Probably her old age messing with her," Sebastian said, his eyes slowly scanning Addy from top to bottom, then back to top.

Oh, if Rick were here.

"I can assure you my mom is not suffering from any sort of dementia," Addy said, clearing her throat, "and neither am I."

"You don't have the right to –" Sebastian said, raising a finger to jab Addy.

Phil swatted his hand away. "I wouldn't do that if I were you."

Addy smiled. At least he had good reflexes. "Why don't we call the police and ask what they think?"

Julian spun, pulling Sebastian behind him. "Yeah, whatever. Good luck with that."

They rushed off, clambering to a van across the street. Both men hopped inside and slammed the doors. In seconds, the van peeled out and disappeared.

Back inside their own car, Mia squealed and Addy burst into laughter.

"I can't believe you did that!"

"I can't either! I don't know what came over me." Mia fanned her face with her hand. "That was crazy."

"They were convinced you were in love with them," Phil said. "You're a great actress."

"Ha, thanks."

"What should we do?" Addy asked. "If I have their names I can file a police report, right?"

"Maybe your mom needs to do it," Mia said. "She'll need to come out here."

Addy sighed. "That's true. Okay, so a little delayed, but we did it! We found those scum bags! They looked *so* guilty."

Mia nodded. "So obvious."

"Wait a minute," Phil said, leaning forward and perching his head between them. "Are you actually an actress? Weren't you in that movie?"

Addy shut her eyes. Rick couldn't get back soon enough.

Sixteen

A round the corner, Sebastian shoved Julian. "I can't believe you were dumb enough to believe she was into you."

"You're one to talk!" Julian rubbed his shoulder, his face twisted, his lips pouting. "You pulled out your driver's license like she was a cop."

"How do we know she wasn't a cop?" Sebastian looked over his shoulder. They were nowhere to be seen, but that didn't mean anything.

"I'm pretty sure if she was a cop, she would've arrested us by now," Julian said.

Sebastian shook his head. "You don't know that."

"She doesn't have anything, man. That old lady gave us the money and there's nothing they can do about it."

"You sure about that?" Sebastian sucked in a shaky breath. "I am not going back to prison over this."

Julian shook his head. "Me neither."

"Do we tell Cliff?"

"No, we don't tell Cliff!" Julian bellowed. "He's going to hit the roof. He's going to tell us to give the money back."

"How much is left?" Sebastian asked.

"What do I look like, a piggy bank? I don't know, man!"

Sebastian pulled out his phone. "I'm going to call Cliff."

"Do not call Cliff!" Julian swatted the phone out of his hand.

"What is your problem?"

His arms were raised and his shoulders tense, like he was getting ready to tackle Julian.

Julian put up his hands. "We can take care of this. She has nothing on us. We'll scare her off."

Sebastian rubbed his face with his hands. "You think we can do that?"

"Yeah. Easy." He scoffed. "Besides, she left us no choice."

Seventeen

His deployment, the nightmares, the pressure on his chest when he woke up – it was all a distant memory in this moment, fading as fast as fog. As he walked through his cousin Cody's hometown, Rick was a kid again.

He'd left the memorial for a short stroll, retracing his childhood steps, floating on the freedom of the endless summer days, running from the movie theater to the public pool to the candy store. Playing baseball in the park. Watching the stars on the trampoline.

As an adult, what did he have to rival that? Life was too complicated. Too many terrible things had happened. What could ever possibly make him feel like summer again?

The candy store was gone, replaced by a vape shop, but the diner stood tall, its light blue booths visible through the window. He used to get milkshakes there with Cody using the money they'd earned mowing lawns.

Rick had his hand on the door of the diner when his chest tightened and he had to bend over, head spinning.

He let go of the door. It was too soon to relive those memories. One day at a time.

Rick strolled back to the memorial. There were twenty people, maybe. His mom was spending most of her time around his aunt, Cody's mom, and everyone spoke in normal tones, snacking and sipping drinks.

A slideshow of Cody played on a screen, shuffling through memories too painful to look at. Cody dressed as a fireman for Halloween. Cody hanging out of a limo at prom. Cody in his army fatigues, his arm around Rick's neck.

When it was over, Rick said his goodbyes and walked back to his car.

His mom followed him there. "Are you sure you're okay?"

"Of course, Mom."

She put her hand on his shoulder. "It's okay to *not* be okay."

He shook his head. "That's not an option."

"Of course it is." Her eyes lingered, searching. "There was nothing anyone could have done. You have to know that."

"Yeah." He pulled her in for a hug. She got smaller every time he saw her. "It was nice to see you."

"I mean it, Rick. You know none of this was your fault, right?"

If only it were that simple.

He kissed her on the cheek. "Love you, Mom. Maybe I can host Thanksgiving this year?"

She laughed. "Now that I would love to see."

He hated to leave her there, standing alone like that. The sting of loss was too acute. He couldn't look at anyone he loved anymore without terror shooting through his bones. Knowing they could, and would, be gone in an instant.

"Are you sure you're okay?" she asked, tilting her head.

He sucked in a breath. "Yeah. I need to get back to work. I'll talk to you soon. Can you call me when you make it home?"

She cracked a small smile. "Yes. We'll talk soon."

The drive back to the Anacortes ferry terminal ran out the clock on his *Mindhunter* book. There were similar books in his queue, but he thought it might be good to take a break from serial killers for a while.

At the same time, what if something more light-hearted couldn't keep his mind occupied? It always went to places he didn't want it to go.

He started the next audiobook, a thriller with a jewel heist and a kidnapping. It kept him busy until the ferry got to San Juan Island.

The ferry was pleasant and, as he drove off the boat, he called Phil. "Where are you guys?"

"We're at the tea shop. Addy's inside with her sister and her mom."

"Where are you?"

"I'm outside. Don't worry, I'm watching the doors."

Rick clenched his jaw. Not good enough. At least he was only a few minutes away. "Everything go all right yesterday?"

"Yeah," Phil said. "Not much going on. She worked a bit. Took the seaplane out –"

"The seaplane? To go where?"

"Oh man, you're not going to believe this. Mia Westwood met up with us. You know, the actress? She's just – *wow*. She's a ten."

"I told you not to leave the island." Rick jerked the wheel onto Turn Point Road.

He thought by taking the car, he'd keep them out of trouble. How could Addy be so reckless?

"I'm just following orders," Phil said, an edge to his voice. "That's what Addy wanted to do."

Rick didn't have an answer. He hung up the phone and shoved it into his pocket.

The tea shop rose into view, like an image from a whimsical postcard. He'd kept imagining this moment and the relief he'd feel when he was back.

Instead, his heart rate picked up. Rick pulled into a spot and shut the car off, jumping out of the driver's seat. Phil stood on the shore, looking out at the water.

Rick had half of mind to shove him into the ocean for being so negligent, but there was more urgent business.

He jogged up to the tea shop and pushed the door open. Marilyn sat in the corner, trapping a woman with wide eyes into a story. Patty was helping customers at the front desk, and Sheila and Addy sat at a table together, heads huddled, voices hushed.

The tension in his chest cracked. She was all right.

Addy looked up, her face lighting with a smile. His breath caught in his throat.

"You're back!" Addy said.

She stood and, for a second, he thought she was going to throw her arms around him.

He braced himself, but no hug came. "I am."

"Is everything okay?" she asked, cocking her head to the side.

"Yeah." He paused. "Actually, no. Phil said you met with Mia yesterday."

She scrunched up her nose. "Busted."

"You told me you were going to stay put," he said.

"I know." Addy sighed. "But Mia found the guys my mom had talked to! We met them in the neighborhood and I got their real names."

Blood rushed in his ears. "You talked to them?"

"Yes, and it was fine. Now we can file a police report and –"

"This isn't a joke, Addy," he said, cutting her off.

She blinked at him. "Nothing happened, Rick."

"It could have." He couldn't control his voice, booming out of him now. "You can't go provoking criminals like that. They could have done something to you. They have nothing to lose."

She waved a hand. "I have to take matters into my own hands sometimes."

"This is exactly what you're not supposed to do," he said.

"I'm not a child, Rick. I can do things." She walked past him, through the door and into the parking lot.

This had nothing to do with her competence and every-thing to do with her safety. Where was this coming from?

He jogged after her. "Where are you going?"

"I need to talk to Chief Hank about this," she said. "Now that you're back, you can come along. I mean, if you're ready to go, you can. If you need some time to decompress –"

"I don't need time to decompress. This is a bad idea. "

She stopped, crossing her arms over her chest. "You think I'm incapable of doing anything, don't you?"

He scoffed. "That's not true. I never said that."

"You're acting like it."

Rick sighed. "I'm here to protect you."

"I don't need to be protected like this! You're treating me like –"

"Like you're being a reckless danger to yourself? Yeah, because you are."

Her face twisted into a scowl. "That's such a Shane thing to say."

She turned and kept walking.

"What are you doing, Addy?"

"I think I can drive myself," she said, raising her voice. She got into her car and slammed the door shut.

He knocked on the window. "Adelaide!"

She pointed a finger to her ear and shrugged. "I can't hear you," she mouthed.

The car reversed and he jumped back. It rolled and rolled, out of the parking lot, rumbling onto the grass, then meandering downhill until it hit a tree with a solid whack.

He ran. "Addy! Are you hurt?"

She dropped the window. "No, I'm fine. My brakes aren't working!" She pushed the pedal down, the sound hollow and sharp.

Of course, Phil wouldn't check her car to make sure it hadn't been tampered with. He was out there looking at the clouds.

Addy turned around, then back to him. "Do you think the tree is hurt?"

He shut his eyes. "Do I think the tree is hurt. I don't care about the tree, Addy. I care about you. I'm not going to lose you too."

She stared at him, her eyes wide.

He looked away, pretending to study the back tires.

Eighteen

It was too much information to take at once. The car, the brakes, the tree.

Rick.

She thought he'd be impressed she'd found the guys. Yes, maybe a bit annoyed that she'd done it without him, but to act like that? And the car...

Addy sat in the driver's seat, her hands frozen on the wheel.

"What was that noise?" Patty shouted, walking out of the tea shop. She shrieked when she saw the car. "Adelaide! Are you okay?"

Sheila ran out, beating Patty to the car. "What happened?"

"I hit the tree," she stammered.

Rick opened the door and reached over her to pull up the emergency brake.

"It's okay," he said softly.

He unbuckled her seat belt and lifted her hands from the steering wheel. "It's okay. Come on out."

Pain shot through her shoulder. She winced, falling into Rick as she put one leg on the ground, then the other.

Her car hadn't randomly broken. The brakes hadn't melted away on their own. They'd *found* her, and they'd cut her brakes, hadn't they?

She released her grip on Rick and looked down, away from his gaze, away from his righteous anger.

Eliza came running, her apron still tied around her waist. "Aunt Addy! What happened?"

"I'm fine," Addy said, nodding. "Everything's fine."

She found herself back in the tea shop, sitting at a table.

Patty carried in a pot of tea. "She's had a shock," she murmured, setting the tea down.

"You forgot how to stop a car?" Marilyn called from across the room, a half-smile on her face.

Sheila poured a cup of tea and pushed it toward Addy. "Mom, that's not funny."

Addy looked up. Eliza had disappeared into the kitchen.

"They cut my brakes," Addy said quietly.

"What? Who cut your breaks?" Sheila asked, leaning in.

Marilyn sighed. "I hope you didn't cause any damage to the car. That's a nice car. You should take care of what you have."

"Thanks, Mom," Addy said, staring at the table.

"I just got it washed and waxed for you," Marilyn added.

The door opened and Rick walked in, his forehead glistening with sweat. His eyes darted back and forth, scanning the room.

"I pushed the car back into a parking spot," he said, slipping into a seat next to Addy. "I'll find someone to tow it. It doesn't look like the tree suffered much damage, but your bumper has a crack in it."

Addy nodded. "Thank you."

"When you talked to those guys," he continued, "did you give them your name? Or where you were staying?"

She shook her head. "No. There's no way they could've found me. It must've been something else. There must have been…" Her voice trailed off.

Rats? Could rats chew through the brake line? Maybe some particularly aggressive sea otters?

Anything except the possibility that she'd behaved like a spiteful teenager to Rick, lashing out at his imagined Shane-isms when all along…he had been right.

"You think someone did this to Addy's car?" asked Sheila, her voice low.

"I know they did," Rick said. "I just don't know who."

Phil walked in, a smile crossing his face when he saw Rick. "Hey man. You're back."

Rick shot to his feet, crossing the room and stopping inches from Phil's face. "Get out of here."

He put his hands up. "Whoa, dude! What's your problem?"

"My problem? It's not my problem, it's yours. You're completely negligent. Adelaide's car was tampered with. Where were you?"

"I was – I thought you were –"

Rick stepped forward, pushing his chest into Phil's space. "Get out of here. Find yourself a new career."

Phil stumbled backwards, catching himself on a chair before skittering out the door.

"That seems a bit dramatic, Rick," Marilyn said. "My Adelaide has always been a terrible driver."

"I got in one car crash when I was seventeen," Addy said. "That doesn't make me terrible driver."

"Looks like *two* car crashes now," she said, pursing her lips. "You really need to be more careful."

Rick turned his fiery gaze onto Marilyn. "If you think –"

Sheila cut him off. "Wait. Mom, what did you say about washing Addy's car?"

"It's my little secret," she said with a smile.

"It's not a secret," Sheila snapped. "Where did you have this done? Who did it?"

"If you must know," she said with a sigh, "I got a call that I'd won a free car wash – a hand wash, mind you – with a custom wax. Now, seeing that I don't have a car at the moment, I thought it would be a nice thing for Addy after she's done so much for me."

Addy shut her eyes. "Mom. You got scammed. Again."

"No, I didn't. The car was cleaned today, wasn't it?"

"What number did they call you from?" Rick demanded.

"I don't know. It said restricted. Now ,I normally don't answer those numbers, but they left me a message telling me I'd won, so –"

"There it is," said Rick. "Your mother handed you to them on a silver platter."

"I didn't hand Addy to anyone," Marilyn said. "I got her a free car wash."

"Mom, they cut my brakes!" Addy said. "Did you tell them where I was staying, too? What else do they know?"

"I just – they didn't do this, I'll have you know."

"What did you say, Mom?" Sheila said sternly.

"I told them her car was outside the tea shop and they should have no trouble finding it."

Addy let out a breath. At least they didn't know where she lived. Maybe.

But were they still around? Watching her? She sat up, glancing around the tearoom.

Eliza walked in at that moment, her jaw dropping. "I'm sorry. I was on the phone, but I heard everything. I can't believe those guys cut your brakes!"

Patty swooped in. "I didn't see any suspicious men around, but when I do…" She slammed her hand on the table. The teacup jumped and clattered back into place.

Addy stood. "I think I need to get some air. Excuse me."

She brushed past Rick and through the back door to the patio. The picnic table sat empty. She wouldn't be able to work there anymore, would she? With the fear of goons looming over her? She'd have to run back to Canada, her tail between her legs…

She took long strides down to the water. When she got there, Rick was two steps behind her.

"I'm sorry about exploding like that," he said. "I didn't mean to scare you."

"You didn't scare me," Addy said, turning to face him. She clutched her shoulder. "I knew what I did was wrong. I was being defensive."

He sighed. "I knew I shouldn't have left."

"No, it's not your fault." She shook her head. "I just...I got it in my head that I needed to figure this out. I needed to prove something."

"You don't have to prove anything to anyone, Addy."

Easy for him to say. He wasn't a washed-up middle-aged divorcée. She wasn't going to get into that now. "I can't believe they found me. And they wanted to..."

She couldn't say the words. She should've listened to Rick. Addy had no idea what she was doing after all.

"I know." He shook his head. "I'm going to find them."

"I was supposed to be in danger from some random group in Canada, yet here I am, stirring up my own trouble like an idiot."

"You're not an idiot," Rick said gently. "You're just trying to help your insufferable mother."

Addy laughed. "Hey."

"I'm sorry." He shook his head. "I can't believe what she did. The danger she put you in."

"She was trying to be helpful, I guess." Addy looked at her feet. The water lapped at the tip of her shoes.

If it were a little warmer, she'd go for a swim. Maybe she still would.

Rick cleared his throat and she looked up at him.

"About what I said. About losing you."

Her chest constricted. She had heard that right. "Have you lost someone before? As a bodyguard?"

A smile flashed across his face. "Not as a bodyguard, no." He turned, looking at the tea shop, then at her. "I went away for a memorial. It was for my cousin Cody."

Her heart sunk. "I'm so sorry. Were you close?"

He nodded. "Cody was six years older than me. I always looked up to him. I never thought..." He shook his head. "After I joined the army, he was inspired to join, too. But after he deployed, he was never the same. He started drinking to deal with the fallout."

Addy stood perfectly still.

Rick went on. "At first, no one wanted to admit it was a problem. He still held onto a job. He was fun to be around. What could I say? I was his little cousin. I never told him what to do. But then..." He shook his head. "I should've said something. I should've done something."

"What happened?"

"He didn't tell any of us, but his liver was failing. I found out when they called me as his emergency contact. He tried to stop drinking and started having seizures."

"Oh, Rick." She wanted to grab his hand. She wanted to pull him in, wrap him up.

"I thought maybe it'd be a wakeup call. I wanted to get him help, but he didn't want to miss work. He stopped answering my calls. I found out he'd gotten evicted from his apartment." He sighed. "I promised I was going to come out again, make him at least talk to me, but he got into a bar fight. He hit his head on the curb and never woke up."

Her eyes flashed with tears. "Rick, I'm so sorry."

"No, I'm sorry. You didn't need to know this," he said.

She grabbed his hand. He squeezed it once before letting go.

"What I'm trying to say..." he trailed off, shaking his head. "That's why I was gone. It was important, but it's over, and I'm not going to leave again, okay? I won't let anything else happen."

"I know." She nodded, staring at him.

His eyes were hard again, looking out at the water.

"We should get back," he said, turning around. "I'm sure everyone's worried about you."

She didn't know what else to say, so she followed him up the hill.

Nineteen

He walked quickly, disguising his gasps for air as exertion. Would Addy notice? The tingling in his hands was fading, but his heart was still racing and his chest was in a vise.

Rick could tell her about Cody. It had been a year. He should be able to talk about it, especially with her.

But Addy couldn't know about this problem of his. This weakness. The shooting pains in his chest. The numbness in his hands. His vision tunneling into darkness.

If Rick thought he was about to die, the decent thing was to keep it to himself.

They reached the tea shop and he pulled the door open for her. He forced a smile, or at least he thought he did.

Inside the tea shop, the air was pleasantly warm and smelled of cinnamon and bergamot. Sheila was shouting at Marilyn. Patty stood with her hands on her hips, watching as Sheila whisked Addy away.

The room kept shifting beneath his feet. Rick took a seat at a table near the door and tried the techniques he'd read on the internet. The feel of his jeans on his hand. One yellow thing he could see. Two red things...

Enough of that. He needed to watch the entrances. The guys could be lurking around. He wasn't going to let anything happen to Addy.

The vise crushing his chest loosened and he took a full breath, then another. He wasn't dying. Not this time.

Just a little panic attack.

As if it being "little" were such a thing. He hated the term. He hated the feeling, the loss of control and the humiliation.

No one seemed to have noticed, though. He'd staved it off for now. Addy couldn't know what a mess he was. She would think –

"If you ever want to talk," she said, appearing at his side, "I'm always here." Then she laughed. "Well, you know that, because you're always here, too."

He forced a laugh. "Ha, yeah. Thanks."

"I mean it, Rick." She raised her eyebrows. "You can't avoid me."

"I know." He looked down.

Stop being weird. Act normal.

Rick looked back up. Her grey eyes were focused on him, as calm as the sea.

She smiled and walked off, back to her seat with Sheila.

By the time he was able to tune in, talks on how to keep Addy safe were well underway.

Rick had his own opinions. It'd be best for Addy to move out of Russell's house, but he knew that wasn't going to happen. He'd have to install cameras. Maybe he could get Iron-

Clad Elite to pay for another bodyguard for more complete coverage? Anyone but Phil. Phil was useless.

Eliza stopped by his table. "Can I get you anything?"

"No. I'm all right, thanks."

She leaned in. "I'm glad you're back. Phil wasn't all there, if you know what I mean."

"I know. He was barely here at all."

Though Phil definitely didn't get panic attacks, making him more useful than Rick...

"I think Aunt Addy is glad you're back, too."

He looked down at the table. "Glad to be back." He hesitated. "Actually, I have a favor to ask you."

"Anything!" Eliza said, grinning.

"Could you get some flyers printed for me? I want the pictures of those guys all over the island."

"I would be honored," she said, hand to her heart.

He laughed. She was a good kid. They were a nice family, even with Marilyn casting the shadow of her ego over everyone.

His family had been a nice family once. It had only taken one tragedy to shatter it to pieces.

He wasn't going to let anything like that happen to Addy.

It was hard to interrupt all the bickering, but eventually he got the pictures of the salesmen's licenses and reached out to his contact to get background. He wanted to know everything about these guys.

Eliza got to work immediately and had a sample ready in thirty minutes. Rick asked her to add **WANTED FOR QUESTIONING** at the top before approving it.

Patty swooped in and said she was friends with the Chief Deputy Sheriff, Hank. She also said his wife Margie knew all the ferry workers and would get the word out.

For the ragtag bunch they were, with a panic-ridden Rick at the helm, their defense came together swiftly. The salesmen wouldn't be able to step foot on the island without being spotted.

Rick was happy with that. It was a good start, but it wasn't enough. He ordered a camera system using the company credit card. It would take two days to get there. That was okay. He didn't plan to sleep.

Through Patty, he secured a mechanic to fix Addy's car. The guy would tow it, fix it up, and bring it back in three days. Top-tier service on this little island.

After two hours, Addy agreed to go back to the house. Once he'd checked the rooms and the property, he let himself relax a little, unlike at the tea shop, where his muscles had been tense and ready to spring with every opening of the door.

Addy didn't seem shaken up anymore. She spent the evening laughing and playing a card game called "Sounds Fishy" with Sheila and Russell. Rick didn't want to join, but they'd insisted they needed one more player. If there had been any sort of real threat, he wouldn't have, but the laughter pulled him in.

The next morning, he heard back from his contact. The salesmen were run-of-the mill petty criminals. Both had spent time in prison. Theft, home break-ins. Check fraud. Witness intimidation. Real stand-up guys.

He called IronClad Elite and told them about the situation and the increased threat to Addy. There was no one higher up to talk to, just someone taking messages, so he said he'd like to discuss more resources for Addy's case.

All there was left to do was sit and wait. They were going to slip up. They would make a mistake and Rick would be there to catch it.

He might not be able to get Marilyn's money back, but he would make them pay. They would go back to prison for what they'd done to Addy.

Maybe then he'd be able to sleep again.

Twenty

Within a week of the brake cutting incident, calm returned to the island. Sheila was suspicious of it. How could people who were willing to do something like that to Addy just...disappear?

Sheila wasn't going to let it go. She kept talking about it, but Addy kept refusing to engage. She brushed off Sheila's concerns, saying that it might have been a tit-for-tat on their part. She had threatened them, they had threatened her. It was over.

Addy had always been optimistic, overly willing to look to the future. It drove Sheila mad sometimes, and it had only worsened with Rick emboldening that little sister of hers.

He installed cameras, motion detectors, and alarms. He hounded the company he worked for and alerted Chief Hank and every officer on the islands. Posters with the guys' faces were up in the grocery stores, at the ferry landing, at the farmer's market. Online, he'd made several threads about the guys and the community was all over them, bubbling with excitement over the drama.

Sheila was grateful for Rick. His stare could be unnerving, and sometimes when she spoke to him he didn't hear her at all, but he took the job of protecting Addy seriously. That was what mattered.

Addy still wanted to do her work at the tea shop, but Rick had put his foot down. It was too risky, and Sheila agreed.

Instead, he set up a table for her on Russell's back deck. It overlooked the water and was more comfortable for working than the lounge chairs.

Sheila did her work there, too. They were only days away from transporting Lottie out to the sea pen, and it was all hands on deck. Mackenzie was working tirelessly from the mainland, making sure everything was moving smoothly and they wouldn't have any surprises. Sheila had gotten pulled into planning some of the welcome festivities.

Working like this was fun, though. It was nice to have time alone with Addy. They hadn't spent this much time together since they were kids.

That's what they were doing, working and enjoying morning coffee, when their mother showed up unannounced.

"I can't believe you wouldn't let me stay here," she said with a sigh. "It's stunning."

"Mom!" Addy stood and gave her a hug. "How did you end up on this side of the island?"

"Lawrence gave me a ride," she said, waving a hand.

"I didn't even hear you sneak up." Sheila set her coffee mug down.

"Don't worry." Rick stepped out from behind her. "I spotted her immediately."

"And you didn't warn us?" Sheila murmured.

He smiled but said nothing.

"How's Lawrence?" Addy asked. "What's he doing on the island?"

"He's helping me move back," Marilyn said simply.

Sheila bit her lip. Could it be true? Was their mother going to leave them alone? "Moving back where?"

"Back to the house," she said with an impatient sigh. "Apparently the whole thing was a misunderstanding, and now we can move back."

"What?" Addy tilted her head. "Who said you could move back?"

"Flex Knock! They called and told me there was a mistake in accounting. They apologized and said we could come back to the house."

"Why would they call you?" Sheila asked. "The contract was under Lawrence."

She scowled. "I didn't come here for a hundred questions. I came here to say goodbye."

"What about your money?" Addy asked. "Did they mention that?"

"No, but I know you're working on it," Marilyn said, picking a piece of fuzz off her coat. "For now, it'd be nice to settle in. It's too loud here and I hate being away from Lawrence."

The poor old sweet man she'd abandoned? Sheila had to clench her teeth to keep her mouth shut.

"I'm happy for you," Addy said slowly, "but it doesn't make a lot of sense. Maybe I should talk to Flex Knock."

"I don't want you messing this up for us," Marilyn snapped. "I'll throw a housewarming party in a month or so and you'll be invited. All right?"

A housewarming party? Sheila and Rick met eyes. They were thinking the same thing. There was no way Addy was going to be going to a housewarming party, not right under the noses of the guys who wanted to hurt her.

Of course, she would insist it was fine.

"Well, best of luck, Mom," Addy said. She gave her another hug.

Sheila got up and gave her one too. "Talk to you later."

"Goodbye, girls! Goodbye, silly little island! I hope I never see you again!"

Island life wasn't for everyone. Sheila was thankful for that.

Once she disappeared, Rick took a seat on the lounge chair.

"Seems suspect," he said. "That suddenly they're letting her move back into the house."

"Yeah..." Addy said, chewing on the cap of her pen. Her eyes were focused in the distance.

"I think your mom is right, though," he continued. "We need to let it go."

She snapped her eyes to him. "What about the money she lost?"

"That money is long gone," Sheila said. "They were probably trying to scare you off, and now they're trying to placate Mom, hoping it'll go away."

Addy frowned. "Maybe."

Sheila shot Rick a look. He was watching Addy with heavy eyes, his lips hard and set. He knew she wasn't going to give it up.

Sheila was more than happy to, though. Their mom had gotten scammed, and that was a real shame, but there was nothing to be done. She had a place to live. She had a nice boyfriend. What more could she want from life?

The real excitement, and the newcomer she'd been waiting for, was about to arrive.

Twenty-one

Whatever the reason Flex Knock had for letting Marilyn and Lawrence back into that house, Rick didn't care. It was a stroke of good luck, and none of them should question it. IronClad Elite was giving him the runaround about getting more resources for Addy, so the further he could get her away from this whole thing, the better.

Naturally, Addy disagreed. The night after Marilyn gave them the good news, she emerged from her bedroom dressed in pajamas and walked into his room, quiet as shadow.

Rick sat on the bed, looking at the new comments from townspeople keeping an eye out for Julian and Sebastian. No one had seen them. He sighed. How had they managed to disappear? And *why?*

"Is everything okay?" Addy asked.

He jumped. "I didn't hear you come in."

"I know." She grinned. "All this time I thought you had super hearing."

"Unfortunately not." If only his eardrums still didn't ring with gunfire. "Is everything okay with you?"

"I don't know. I guess so. I can't stop thinking about my mom getting back in the house."

"Because you're so grateful?" he suggested, a half smile tugging at his mouth.

"No, because it doesn't make any sense. Clearly they're giving in to her, which means whatever we're doing is working."

He shut his laptop. "Not necessarily. You're letting yourself be influenced by what you want to be true."

Addy crossed her arms. "It's not that simple and you know it, Rick."

"I didn't say it was simple, I –"

"Let me finish," she said, holding up a finger.

He sat back. He was not winning this one.

She went on. "Flex Knock had already gotten them out of the house. Why would they let them move back in, unless they felt threatened in some way? It's no benefit to them."

He sighed. "It could be any of a number of reasons."

"Yeah, but you know it isn't. You have to trust me sometimes, you know. Just because you're the bodyguard and I'm the client doesn't mean I don't know anything."

The client. He hadn't thought of her as "the client" in ages. "I'm sorry. I don't think of you as not knowing anything. I never meant to treat you that way, and I'm really sorry."

Her lips twisted into a frown. "You don't have to apologize, I just – I want you to take me seriously."

Rick was taking her seriously. He knew she wouldn't give this up, and he desperately needed her to. "My first priority is to protect you, always." He paused. There was no need to reiterate that he didn't want to lose her; no reason for her to know she was becoming less "the client" and more the focus of his every thought. "You have a different first priority, which puts us at odds."

"True." She dropped her arms. "There has to be more to it, though. How do we know they won't throw them out of the house again in six months? Then we're back where we started."

"You're right. I'm still working on getting the guys to talk, and my contacts are looking for ways in," he said. "I haven't given up."

A smile curled her lips and she took a step toward him. "Oh. I didn't know that."

His heart danced against his ribs, distinct from the feeling of a panic attack. Far more pleasant, like the fluttering of a dove's wings.

He cleared his throat. "I don't want you putting yourself in harm's way to figure this out. It's too personal. They can come after you, but they can't come after a nameless, faceless investigator. Or the cops."

"Specifically Chief Hank."

He smiled. "Yeah. He's on it."

"All right. Well, I'm glad we talked it through."

"Me too."

The lighting softly lit her eyes, her nose, her lips...

Addy nodded, then turned on her heel. "Sleep tight, Rick!"

He watched her disappear behind her door. "Thanks. You too."

If only she knew how well he slept when she was near.

• • •

There was nothing from Marilyn for the next week, and Addy was distracted by the chaos in the house. Lottie the orca was finally coming home.

Rick had never seen Sheila in such a state.

"Eliza!" she barked on the morning of transport. "Can you add four people to the afterparty?"

"No problem," Eliza said. "I made extra of everything."

"We need to make sure everyone who comes and who volunteers has something to eat and a hot drink –"

Patty cut her off. "Don't worry. We've got it under control."

Sheila's eldest daughter, Mackenzie, arrived that morning, along with her boyfriend, Liam. Mackenzie was even more frightening than Sheila.

"Joey!" Mackenzie called across the kitchen. "I've got press pickups in Bellingham, Seattle, and Tacoma."

"Got it," he said.

"Listen, if you can't fit Tacoma in, that's fine, but the one in Seattle is from a national news network and we *need* them at the sea pen."

Joey nodded, chewing on a cookie. "They'll be there, boss."

Russell was already at the sea pen site, drumming up interest. Chief Hank was coming to give them a boat ride any minute. He was also providing security for the event and making sure no unwanted visitors caused trouble.

He pulled up in the police boat and welcomed them. Rick shook his hand. "Nice to see you again."

"You too, Rick." He hopped onto the dock to help Patty carefully step onboard. "How goes the bodyguard business?"

"It's been quiet recently. Still no sign of my guys?"

Hank shook his head. "I'm keen to get my hands on them. If I could get them in for questioning, I could get at least one of them to squeal. "

Rick grinned. "I believe it."

He stepped to the back, taking his place next to Addy.

"I don't know if Hank looks as tough as he talks." Addy tilted her head, squinting behind her sunglasses. "From what Patty tells me, he's a softie."

"Who says a softie can't be tough?"

She laughed. "I guess you're right. You're a softie, and you're pretty tough."

"There's your mistake." He crossed his arms over his chest and leaned back on the boat's railing. "I'm just tough."

"Ha! Yeah, sure."

Once they were loaded onto the boat, Hank skillfully maneuvered away from the dock, past the rows of boats in Friday Harbor and on to Stuart Island.

It was Rick's first time seeing the sea pen site. It was as breathtaking as the rest of the islands, with the addition of a quaint fisherman's village built at the shore.

Addy had told him all about how Russell had set this into motion – not that he would take any credit for it. He seemed to be an effective fundraiser and point of contact, however.

They'd taken over an old fisherman's lodge and converted the buildings into veterinarians' quarters, a dining hall, and guest rooms. In the open water offshore, the edges of a three hundred by two hundred foot sea pen bobbed in the waves.

The scale of it was incredible. Rick gaped mouth open, shutting it only when he realized Liam was recording all of them on camera.

"Sorry, mate," Liam said, patting him on the shoulder.

"No, it's me." Rick shook his head. "I can't believe this is all for a whale."

"Is it, though?" Liam squinted, wiping crops of water from his sunglasses before replacing them. "It's not just for Lottie. It's for all the whales pulled from these waters and slaughtered. The ripple through the generations of these families."

"What do you mean?"

"The whales. They live with their families their entire lives. Eighty, a hundred years. Like people." Liam shook his head. "Honestly, I'm starting to sound like Russell. But taking Lottie away devastated her mother and her sisters. They're in for the shock of their lives when they hear her calls again."

Rick could only offer a nod and a grunt. Behind his black sunglasses, his eyes were strangely reacting to the wind.

The dock was crowded with boats, but Hank found a spot. Russell rushed to meet them.

"Don't worry, Mackenzie," he said quickly when he caught her scowl. "Everyone who's here is allowed to be here."

"Good, because I will kick out any party crashers."

He laughed. His face was lit with a smile. "I can't believe it's finally here."

"How's Lottie doing?" Sheila asked. "When did you last hear from the vets?"

"Half an hour ago. She's doing well," Russell said. "Getting her into the sling was a bit stressful. She was calling out a lot when they lifted her into the air, but once they got her into the portable tank, she calmed down."

They walked along the shore and to the lodge. There was a gaggle of people, talking and laughing, and a woman was spooning out hot cider.

"Hello, hello!" she called out.

Rick didn't realize he was getting a mug until she was standing in front of him, shoving it into his hands.

"You must be Rick!" She grinned, hands on her hips. "I'm Margie, Hank's wife."

"Hello. I've heard so much about you."

"You have to have the cider," she said. "It's from a fantastic farm on Orcas Island. A friend of mine has a hotel there. Have you been?"

"No, I haven't."

"I'll have to take you on a field trip," Addy said with a smile. "Hi, Margie."

"Addy! I can't believe that business with your car. Do you have pepper spray? I can get you some pepper spray—it's very effective if you just aim and shoot."

"I don't need pepper spray." She clapped a hand to Rick's shoulder. "I've got a personal bodyguard."

Rick laughed. "Pepper spray is still a good idea."

Patty stole Margie away, and he was left sipping hot cider with Addy.

"I heard you sent Mia pepper spray," she said.

"Yeah?" He stared off into the distance, pretending to think. "Nah. That must've been another Rick."

"No, pretty sure it was you. That was nice. It almost makes up for you fleeing the car in terror when she burst into tears."

He laughed. Not his proudest moment. He wouldn't do the same now. "That was a different Rick, too."

"There they are!" Eliza yelled, pointing.

The crowd hushed, searching the sea. A boat bumbled toward them, the hum of its engine slow and steady.

"How's this going to work?" Rick asked.

"Well, Lottie is in a little tank on that barge. See that other boat, here?"

He nodded. He'd seen it when they arrived, a crane sitting stationary.

"They have her in a sling. The crane will lift her up and into the pen."

"What? That's insane."

She shrugged. "That's what they have to do. She weighs eight thousand pounds."

Within minutes, the barge with Lottie arrived. Rick couldn't see her – she was surrounded by people dumping ice and clipping straps. A few were inside the tank with her.

The barge maneuvered as close to the crane as possible, and the long arm dropped. Two people leapt into action, securing hooks. Then the crane started moving.

Lottie emerged from the little container, her tail hanging limp from the sling, two wetsuit-clad women on either side. Her black skin was dull.

"Why does she look like that? Is she sick?"

"No, they put ointment on her skin," Addy said. "To keep her from drying out."

Whale problems.

They rose twenty feet up and everyone stood, silent, watching.

Whistles and clicks rang through the air.

"Is that her?" Rick asked.

Addy nodded, grinning. "Yeah, she's a talker."

He wondered what she was saying. Probably something like "Put me down!"

The crane slowly lowered Lottie into the pen. Another team swarmed the sling, blocking it from view and working as efficiently as an F1 pit stop team.

It took half an hour to remove the sling, but as soon as it was done, all the helpers parted and scattered. Lottie lifted her head from the water, let out a blow, and disappeared beneath the surface.

Everyone stood on the edge of the shore, watching breathlessly. Twenty feet away, Lottie emerged, blowing a great breath. They cheered.

She popped her body above the water, splashing down onto her side.

Rick felt a pair of arms around him. It was Sheila, tears streaming down her face. "She made it!"

He squeezed her back. "It's amazing."

A guy he didn't know grabbed him next. Rick laughed, returning the hug and patting him on the back. "Great work, whoever you are."

He stepped back. Addy stood in front of him. She put her arms up. Her eyes were red with tears, and her face was wide with a grin.

Until now, he'd held it together, but looking at her, a ball tightened in his throat. He bit his lip and leaned in, wrapping his arms around her body.

Addy tightened her grip. Her hair smelled of flowers. He closed his eyes.

"I'll admit it. She's the most beautiful thing I've ever seen," Rick said in her ear.

"Softie," she muttered.

Twenty-two

Had that hug lingered? Or was Addy imagining things?

It couldn't be. Rick was her *bodyguard*. He was contractually obligated to care about her physical safety. He wasn't hugging her because he liked her. It was polite. He'd even hugged that weird guy who had vodka spewing from his pores.

The fact that Rick had pretty eyes and a gruff smile and that he looked handsome in a simple black t-shirt was beside the point. She wasn't supposed to notice these things! She was forty-eight years old. She wasn't supposed to be developing a crush.

She hadn't had a crush in decades. Had she even found another man attractive in any recent memory?

Addy had to stop to consider. There was the occasional movie with a hot new star, but that wasn't anything real. Nothing she felt in her chest, the weight that hit her when Rick walked in a room.

Had there ever been anyone at work? No. She'd been, maybe foolishly, quite happy in her marriage. Dealing with a crush was an entirely new problem.

When had this nonsense of a crush started? Was it when he'd sprinted off the dock and rescued Mia like a ninja? After he swooped in during Patty's ill-arranged blind date? Or was it just hours ago, when she saw him watching Lottie and his eyes misted with tears?

Her heart leapt at the memory.

It didn't matter. She was too old for crushes and on top of that, Rick was too young for her to have a crush on!

After the hug, Addy managed to avoid Rick's gaze, talking to strangers and gushing over the miracle of Lottie's safe arrival. Sheila, Russell, and Mackenzie rushed off to talk to the team, and Hank volunteered to take them back to the tea shop for the afterparty. Addy gladly accepted.

Eliza and Patty had organized a beautiful spread, made for grazing people to come and go as they pleased. It was a joyous event. Addy talked to researchers, veterinarians and some of Russell's Hollywood contacts about what a big project this had been.

"I'm impressed by everything," Rick said, leaning in. He had a plate of finger sandwiches in his hand, and offered it to Addy.

Her stomach flipped and she shook her head. "I'm good, thanks."

"I don't mean any offense by this." He popped a cucumber sandwich into his mouth. "But it's a lot for a whale."

"Don't let anyone hear you say that!" Addy said, looking over her shoulder.

"I didn't say it wasn't worth it. It's the most wholesome thing I've ever seen."

His gaze was fixed on her. He smiled, dimple aglow.

Addy looked down. "I know what you mean. I think it's about righting a wrong."

"Oh, I know. Liam told me about it, and I get it now. I do." He looked up, pausing, his lips slightly parted. "I tried talking to Russell, too, but he started rambling about wolves and I wasn't able to follow."

"Ha, yeah. Russell loves wolves. He's fascinated by their personalities and their pack dynamics."

"Every wolf matters to the pack, right?"

Addy nodded. She'd heard this more than once, and all about Russell's love for Wolf 8. "They do."

Who was Addy's pack? Would she ever matter to anyone again? She mattered to Riley. Maybe that was all she needed – to realize this, to let the gratitude run through her.

"Righting a wrong, too," Rick said. "Cody used to say something like that. He loved cats. He was always bringing home boxes of kittens people had abandoned. Feeding them every three hours around the clock."

"That's so sweet."

"It was. He said you can't change the world, but you can change the world for one kitten."

Addy sighed. "He's right."

"He was a good guy. He had problems, but he had a good heart."

"It sounds like it." Before she could stop herself, Addy's hand was on his arm. "He was very dear to you, wasn't he?"

He patted her hand and nodded. "Yeah. It was frustrating at times, watching him do what he did. Drink himself into a stupor. Lose jobs. Lose girlfriends, people who really cared about him. But..." Rick looked up, eyes searching. "He was still Cody. He'd be flat broke, out of work, and he'd send me a picture of a new cat."

Addy smiled. She wanted to say something poignant, something kind, but then the front door sprung open and Mackenzie walked in. "We did it!" she yelled.

The room erupted into cheers, and the moment was lost in the chaos.

· · ·

Not one to spoil her first crush in centuries, Addy found a way to add to the awkwardness the next day.

It was a slow-moving accident she should've seen coming, but didn't. She was too focused on cornering Sheila.

"You said you wanted to do this," Addy said, wagging a finger in Sheila's face, "and I booked it! You can't back out now."

"Why don't you take Patty?" Sheila suggested.

"I highly doubt Patty wants to climb in or out of a kayak," Addy said.

"What are you guys talking about?" Rick asked, tearing his attention away from the coffee pot.

"Nothing," Addy said.

"Addy is angry at me because I'm too busy to go on her bioluminescence kayak tour tonight."

Addy sighed. "I booked it a month ago! They said your best chance of seeing the glow is under a dark moon—hence tonight—and I didn't want to miss out."

"I didn't know it would be the day after Lottie got here," Sheila said. "I'm sorry. I just can't make it. Maybe Eliza will go."

Rick was watching with too much interest. This should have been Addy's first clue, but she was too intent on not seeing it to notice.

"It's fine," Addy waved a hand. "I'll reschedule."

Sheila narrowed her eyes. "You said there are no refunds, though."

Addy glared at her. "I can reschedule."

Sheila blinked, then looked around the room. A smile tugged at the corner of her lips.

No, no, no. That wasn't a good look.

"What about..." Sheila said, smiling, "Rick? I bet he's good at kayaking."

He took a swig of coffee. "I bet I am."

Addy glared at her. Sheila pretended not to notice.

"It's really okay," Addy said, rushing to wipe crumbs off the counter.

There was no way she was going on a romantic kayak tour with Rick after having all those confusing feelings about him. It wasn't happening. She would put her foot down. She'd burn the tickets.

"It's a date!" Sheila said with a grin. She clapped them both on the shoulder. "Have fun, you two!"

Addy shut her eyes.

"Should we get dinner first?" Rick asked, slipping into the spot next to her, mug of coffee in hand. "There's that fish and chips place we pass all the time but never get to try."

She let out a weak laugh. "Oh, yeah. I guess we could."

It was hard to say what was worse. Addy flying into a full panic around her newly minted crush? Or said crush being so uninterested in her that he didn't even consider the impropriety of a romantic late-night cruise?

"Or we can go somewhere else. Burgers?"

Romantic burgers. Of course.

Clearly, there was nothing there. Only her own whipped up feelings. If she could find a way to ignore the crush, it would certainly go away.

"Let's try the fish and chips," she said, turning to look him in the eye. "That'll be nice."

She looked back at the counter and collected a stray crumb, her heart pounding as she walked it to the sink.

Twenty-three

He knew he wasn't her first choice to take on the kayak tour, but Rick was thrilled. Not that he cared much for kayaking – that seating position made his hips ache – but he was excited to do something with Addy.

She'd been busy recently, and he'd missed her insightful comments. He missed the way she looked up when she was thinking, then the way his heart sped when her gaze fell back on him...

At dinner, Addy was quiet, forcing Rick to lead the conversation.

"What's next for you after San Juan Island?" he asked.

She shrugged. "To be honest, I haven't thought about it."

"Really? You're such a planner."

"Normally I am, but with the divorce, it feels like the rug was pulled out from under me. I'm still figuring out where to start."

To Rick, it seemed like she always knew what she was doing. He wondered if he seemed that way to other people. What a fabrication that was. "How are the translations going?"

"Surprisingly well." A smile finally lit her delicate features. "Just when I think I've reached the end of the line, I get a new client. Then another, then another. My clients keep referring me to people they know, which is…" She shook her head. "So incredibly flattering."

Rick grinned. "I think you've created your dream job."

"You have no idea. I never thought someone like me could make a living this way."

"Someone like you?"

She rolled her eyes. "You know. A boring mom. Someone who thought her job at the university was so lowly that she'd be safe. I was wrong about that, too."

"You're not boring, Addy."

She shrugged. "I try to stay useful."

Did she really believe these things about herself? Shane had done a number on her. Or maybe it was just a boring marriage, because Addy certainly wasn't boring.

"You're a businesswoman. An entrepreneur."

"Yeah," she scoffed, "I'm a real Andrew Carnegie."

He laughed. "The most exciting thing about your new job is you can do it anywhere. Even Italy."

She took a bite of her french fries. "Wouldn't that be nice."

"What's stopping you?"

"Not being insane, I guess?"

He smiled. "Something to think about."

Addy stood from her seat, stacking their empty baskets onto a tray. "We should get going. I don't want to be late."

Rick nodded and stood. He wasn't going to argue with her, but it seemed like Addy was living inside an invisible box.

Invisible to her, at least. Maybe it used to be there, blocking her in. Maybe her ex-husband put walls around her, or maybe her mother had, or society in general. She'd lived inside the box dutifully for many years.

But now the box was gone. There was nothing to keep her contained, save for her instinctive recoil whenever she got close to where the boundaries used to be.

There had to be a way to show her she was anything but boring, that she didn't have to be useful to be worthwhile.

If only Rick had the words...

They got back in the car and drove to the launch site. The sun had started to set, and the sky was kissed with pinks and reds, darkness quickly falling. Rick shone a flashlight on the steep, wooden stairs down to the beach, fighting the urge to hold Addy's hand on the way down.

There were four other people going on the tour, plus the guide. They stood on the beach, sinking into the rocks, and listened to the guide talk about safety, then the wonder of the sea.

After getting dressed in the kayak spray-skirts and life vests, Rick helped drag all the kayaks to the edge of the water. He and Addy were assigned a two-person kayak. He held it steady as she stepped in.

"I don't want you to hurt your shoulder," Rick said. "So I forbid you from paddling."

"I have to paddle!" she said. "I have to pull my weight!"

He pushed the kayak out slightly, hopping in once they were clear. The icy water was above his knees. "You can pull your weight by taking pictures."

"I don't know why, but I'm nervous," she said, a giggle escaping her as they took off. "Is it cold? It feels cold."

Rick's arms were already warm from paddling. He should've worn short sleeves. "It's cold."

He followed the guide as best as he could, avoiding any prolonged gazes at the endless dark sea. The fact that anything or anyone could be hiding in the darkness made his skin tingle.

Within minutes, the water lit up around them. At first it was a few glimmers of light, but soon every stroke of the paddle glowed a bright, electric blue.

The kayaks around them cut through the water, splashing and thrashing, a stunning dance in the stark black night.

"This is incredible!" Addy whispered. She plunged her paddle into the water, ripping it back and forth in a bright blue blast.

Rick laughed. He splashed his paddle forward, the blue arch of water gracefully collapsing beside her. Her face was lit for the briefest of moments, her smile wide and laughing.

Maybe Addy would never leave the island. The trial could drag on for years. They could live here where no one else could find them. Rick could settle for this paradise.

• • •

A call early the next morning cut his dream short. It was his boss at IronClad Elite.

"Morning," Rick said, toothbrush hanging from his mouth.

"Hey, Rick. Good news. Your contract is up. You can go home."

"What?" He shifted the phone to his other ear. He must've misheard. "It can't be up. I asked for more resources, not to be released. There are issues here. Safety and –"

"You don't need anything else. We've determined the threat is over. You can return the car by the end of the week, and you'll be paid for the rest of the month."

"That doesn't make any sense. Is the trial over?"

"I don't ask questions, man. I just carry out the orders, and you should do the same."

Rick spit into the sink. "I'm the one on the ground here. I know what's going on, and the threat isn't over."

"This isn't a negotiation. End of the week."

Click.

Sweat sprung on his forehead. Rick looked at himself in the mirror. His skin was pale, drained of blood.

He turned on the water to warm his hands. Who was going to look out for Addy if they sent him away? Why were they doing this? Were they trying to punish him for speaking up?

His chest heaved with breaths, each one more difficult than the last.

"Oh Rick!" Addy called through the door. "Did I catch you still snoozing, sleepy head?"

He cleared his throat. "No, I'm up. I'll be out in a minute."

"I'm going to head downstairs."

"Sounds good." He'd never not been there when she opened the door. She would know something was up. He had to act fast.

Think, think.

If IronClad Elite wasn't going to stand behind him, he had to find someone who would. Who would have the power and influence to do anything? Unless...

He searched for Addy's husband online. Judge Shane Ashbourne. He was easy to find, a picture of his unnaturally dark hair and stern gaze front and center. The phone number for his office was right there.

It was the fastest he was going to be able to talk to someone about this. Rick dialed.

"Judge Ashbourne's office, how can I direct your call?"

"Hi, this is Rick Hayle. I'm providing personal security for Judge Ashbourne's ex-wife Adelaide Ashbourne. I have urgent security concerns I need to discuss with him. "

"He's in a meeting right now, but I'll take down your information and get it to him right away."

The muscles in his chest eased. He let out a breath. "Thank you."

He explained IronClad Elite wanted to sever his contract, but he had concerns, especially with a recent attack on Addy's safety.

After hanging up, he took a few deep breaths. The judge would call him back. They would sort this out. It would be okay.

The smell of toasting bread drifted into his room. He opened the door and walked down the stairs, counting as he went, grounding himself.

"Good morning," Addy said.

"Good morning," he said back, his voice controlled.

Coffee. That would steady his hands. They were shaking a little. Addy couldn't see that. A pot was already brewing. He grabbed a mug.

"Did you have sweet dreams of glowing water?"

He jumped a little. She was talking to him. "Ha, yeah. Did you?"

"No, in my dreams I was having lunch at an Italian café. It was sunny, and I had a cappuccino and a pastry." She paused. "Pretty boring, but maybe it was a dream of heaven."

He smiled. "Maybe."

Her phone rang and she grabbed it from the counter. "Hello?" Her brow furrowed. "What? I didn't hear anything about this."

Rick stared at her, his arm frozen, holding his mug, his heartbeat pounding in his ears.

"Hang on, that doesn't make any sense." Addy turned to him. "Rick, my ex-husband is saying he got a call from someone concerned about my safety?"

Rick cleared his throat. "I called him, yes. IronClad Elite severed my contract today and I needed to fix it."

She held up a finger, indicating for him to wait. He clenched his teeth, focusing on his breaths. One in, one out. Two in, two out.

Addy listened, biting her lip. "Okay, well, like I said, I didn't know about it but –" She sighed. "All right, it's not my fault that –"

She stopped again. The guy wouldn't let her get a word in.

"Let her talk!" Rick bellowed.

She set the phone onto the kitchen counter. "He had to go."

"He was supposed to call me back. I need to talk to him. This is unacceptable."

"What's unacceptable is that you didn't talk to me first. I didn't know you'd set me up for an angry phone call from my ex-husband about how I need to be more responsible."

"That's ridiculous," Rick said. "He needs to –"

She cut him off. "Why did you go behind my back?"

"I didn't go behind your back," he said. "I needed to talk to someone immediately who had power to do something about this."

"That's not it." She dropped her hands to her sides. "You treat me like I have no idea what's going on. You're no better than he is."

"Come on," Rick said. "You can't be serious."

"Now he thinks I'm sitting here, scared to death. He told me to grow up."

"You should be scared. You were threatened. You –"

"I'm not going to be scared, Rick! If they think the threat is gone, maybe the threat is gone. Maybe it was never there to begin with."

"But it was. It *is*," Rick stammered. "What are you saying? Do you want me to go?"

"I – that's not what this is about."

It was too late. His chest was a vise. No air was getting in, no matter how hard he fought. He shut his eyes. Addy could not see him like this. He turned, pushed the front door open, and walked out.

Twenty-four

Huh, so that was it. He was really going to walk out on her like that.

Addy picked up the frying pan and slammed it onto the stove. She spun, pulling at the fridge, glasses clanking in the door.

She shoved the milk aside. Where were the eggs? Were they seriously out of eggs?

Shane had spoken to her like she was a child. A scared child, telling her to grow up, to stop making this about her. She slammed the door shut.

"Is everything okay?" Sheila asked, standing at the end of the kitchen island.

Addy looked up. "Everything's wonderful. Why?"

"You look like one of those women photographed in the Dust Bowl during the depression."

She was just hungry.

Sheila took a step closer. "Where's Rick?"

"Rick's gone."

Sheila looked around as if she didn't believe it. "Gone where?"

"I don't know and I don't care."

Sheila crossed her arms over her chest. "Aw, a lover's quarrel?"

"Not lovers, Sheila!" Addy snapped. "We had a professional disagreement."

Except it didn't feel professional. It felt like she wanted to throw up. Her ears were hot and her sweater was too tight.

Sheila put her hands up. "I'm sorry. I'm just kidding."

Addy sighed. "I don't know if it's a disagreement. He decided to tell everyone except me that his protection contract had ended."

"Hang on. He's not going to be your bodyguard anymore?" Sheila's mouth dropped open. "How does that make sense? I thought he was trying to get more help out here, not less."

"That's what he told us he was doing, but who knows what he actually did?" Addy pulled two slices of bread from the toaster. They were hard and cold. She tossed them into the sink.

"What did that bread ever do to you?" Sheila asked, biting her lip.

Addy cracked a smile. "Nothing. I forgot about it when I was arguing with Rick and now it's gross."

Plus one of them had been for Rick, but he wasn't going to need it. He'd gotten his walking papers and stormed off.

"So he told you he was pulled off the assignment and walked out? Just like that?" Sheila scrunched her nose as though something stank. "That doesn't seem like him."

"He didn't tell me anything. I got a call from Shane. He was livid that he had to hear about this at all, then blamed me for being dramatic."

"Wait, heard about it from who?"

Addy put her hands over her face. "Rick. He called Shane and told him it was inappropriate for the company to end his contract, that I needed to be protected. "

"Oh." Sheila nodded slowly. "I see where this is going."

The tightness in her chest eased. Finally, someone was listening to her.

Addy took a breath. "Yeah. Then Shane called and scolded me, told me I'm a child, and said he's done indulging me."

Sheila's eye twitched. "He said *what?*"

"I know." Addy shook her head. "It's embarrassing, but maybe he's right."

"No, he isn't! Your brakes were *cut*. Those guys are after you, Adelaide."

"Yeah, and that was my own fault," Addy said. "Apparently, if I leave them alone, they'll leave me alone, too. It had nothing to do with Shane's case. None of that even mattered."

"Shane's being a jerk and you know it. He's always done stuff like this. He's probably having a bad day and took it out on you."

Addy stared at the floor. He had sounded very annoyed, and he was terrible at handling his emotions. To everyone else, he was a stoic judge, ruler of all, but to Addy, he was a man who couldn't deal with getting the wrong cheese at a restaurant.

"I said gorgonzola," he'd once hissed through gritted teeth. "What's the point of going out to eat and paying for things when you don't even get what you want?"

He could be ridiculous sometimes.

"Shane's the child. You know this," Sheila said gently. "Don't let him get to you. Not anymore."

Rick had treated her like a child, too. Going over her head, excluding her.

She'd thought he was different. She'd thought he'd seen her for who she was.

Ah, unless...

Maybe he did see her for who she was, and that person couldn't be trusted. She was foolhardy, and reckless, and...

"I can't believe Rick called him," she went on, shaking her head. "We were arguing about it and he just turned and walked out the door." She walked to the window and peered out. "His car is gone, too. I guess he's done with me."

"I'm sure he's not done with you. Why don't you call him?"

Addy rolled her eyes. "I'm not going to call him. He can apologize when he's ready."

A smile crept across Sheila's face. "Looks like this is about something else."

"No, it isn't. It's about respect."

Sheila did a little dance with her shoulders. "Respect. Right."

Addy stared at her. "What are you getting at?"

"I think you wouldn't be *this* upset about him if you didn't care about more than just respect. I've seen the way you two look at each other. You went on that romantic kayak excursion and came back as giddy as two kids after a night at a theme park."

Addy put a hand up. "I'm not having this conversation."

"All right, that's fine." Sheila cackled a laugh. "I have to run anyway. Joey's flying me to Seattle. I'm supposed to record three more songs for my album today."

Addy sucked in a breath. "Are you serious? Can I come? Or at least hear the songs?"

Sheila shook her head. "I'm not ready to share. The album will only be done if they're good. If they're not good, then people can wait."

"I thought you needed to get the album done before Russell's movie came out?"

She pulled her coat on. "I do. I mean, I'm supposed to, but you can't rush art."

Addy smiled. Such integrity, her sister. Addy always admired her for it. "Well, good luck. I'm rooting for you."

Russell came downstairs, rushing by to put on his coat and catch a ride to Stuart Island.

Addy was on her own.

. . .

She hadn't been alone in weeks and, to be honest, it wasn't all it was cracked up to be.

Outside, the sky hung above her head, a monotone gray. There was no sign of the sun. She got in her car and drove to town, parking in an open spot on the street.

She walked until she found a café overlooking the harbor. Addy walked up the wooden stairs, and inside the cozy warmth of the shop, ordered a breakfast sandwich and the tea latte of the month.

It came out quickly and she sat at a cold metal table outside, enjoying the beautiful drink drizzled with caramel, whipped cream, and cinnamon.

Her napkins kept trying to escape in the wind. She weighed them down with her phone, then picked up the breakfast sandwich. A bagel, egg, and cheese for $14. The beautiful drink had been an extra six.

Her phone rang out and her heart leapt. It had to be Rick. "Hello?"

The napkins took off, dancing on a gust.

"Hey, Addy. It's Mia."

She really needed to start looking at who was calling before she answered. "Hey, Mia. How are you?"

"Good," she said slowly. "Hoping you won't be mad at me."

Addy smiled and took a sip. It tasted like fall. Maybe once in a while it was okay to get a six-dollar drink if it warmed her like this. "I doubt that will happen. What's up?"

"Well, I didn't want to tell you about this unless it panned out, but I think it has panned out." Mia cleared her throat. "I have this friend from college who became a private investigator."

"Okay." This was going to take a while. Addy took a bite of sandwich. It was good, but she liked her own sandwiches more. And the ones she made didn't cost $14.

"He's an interesting guy. He was a programmer and worked in cybersecurity for a while, but he transitioned into being a private investigator. Not a traditional one, though. He's a digital private investigator."

"Digital," Addy repeated.

"Yeah, like, everything he does is online."

Another bite. The bacon was a nice addition. "Oh."

"I asked him to look into your guys and Flex Knock."

She set the sandwich down. "Did he find something?"

"Yes, but the way he found out may not have been entirely legal, if you know what I mean."

A laugh escaped from Addy. "Am I part of a crime?"

"No, nothing like that. Let's just say he found the owner of Flex Knock, saw his bank statements, and found out he likely paid off a judge."

"A judge?" She sat up. "What was the judge's name?"

"Judge Kearn," Mia said.

"Oh." She settled back into her seat. Not Shane. Even a midlife crisis wouldn't make him accept bribes.

"He ruled on a case where Flex Knock was being sued for unfair business practices, and guess what? Flex Knock won."

"Of course."

"Your two guys were involved! Their accounts cleared a lot of money."

"That's interesting."

"Yeah, likely money laundering. At least, that's how it looks." Mia was speaking faster now, her words running together. "My PI was able to get access to their text messages, too."

"Should I even ask how?"

"Better not," Mia said, "but what's important is that they said where they stashed your mom's money."

Her heart jumped. "Where is it?"

"It's at the office for a boating insurance company, which the owner of Flex Knock also owns. It's called Lighthouse Bay."

"Lighthouse Bay," Addy repeated. She needed to commit that to memory. Rick would want to know and –

Wait. Except he wouldn't. Her heart sank. Addy set her sandwich down, her stomach rolling.

Mia spoke again. "They've had a lot of lawsuits dismissed against them. The office is in Bellingham if you wanted to check it out."

Addy bit her lip. She shouldn't do it. Rick wouldn't approve.

Then again, Rick was nowhere to be found. He'd gone behind her back and left her to fend for herself.

She could do this. She could stop by, casually look around, figure out what was going on. She was capable of doing this by herself. Shane and Rick might not believe it, but she did.

"Where was the money being hidden?"

"There's a safe, apparently. They texted each other the combination."

A laugh escaped from Addy. "You're kidding."

"I'm not. They argued over where eight thousand ended up, but it seems like the rest is still there."

This was too good to be true. She could put an end to this, once and for all.

"Can you send that to me? The address and the combination?"

Mia squealed. "You're not mad?"

"Not at all. Thank you. I'm going to get right on this."

"Yay!" Mia let out a sigh. "Please assure Rick this guy I'm working with is legitimate. Uh, even if some of his techniques aren't."

"Sure," Addy said, picking up her plate and mug. "He won't mind anyway."

Twenty-five

G etting in the car had been a mistake, but Rick didn't have any other option. He couldn't let Addy see what was about to happen.

By the time he got out of the house, he was gasping for air. He pulled open the driver's door as his heart pounded against his ribs, pain shooting across his arms and chest in twisted vines. He could feel his pulse at the end of every nerve.

Rick shut the door, heat and nausea retching inside his gut. He put a numb hand to his stomach as his body shook and rattled.

The world was soundless and muffled, like he was being pulled under water. The walls of the car were closing in like a casket.

He was going to die this time. He was sure of it. His heart would finally give out and they'd find him cold and lifeless, slumped against the steering wheel.

The fact that Addy hadn't come after him was a godsend. The fear of her seeing him only prolonged the panic, but in the privacy of the car, the most intense symptoms stopped after fifteen minutes.

Once his body had stopped shaking, Rick managed to pull out of the driveway and park behind the tea shop. Thankfully, no one seemed to be looking for him.

He put an unsteady hand into the glove compartment and fished out a candy bar. It was there for emergencies only. He'd hoped it wouldn't be his own, but alas. Maybe he knew he'd be the one needing it when he'd bought it.

He hadn't died this time, but it was the final nail in his coffin. He had to go. Rick couldn't protect Addy. He couldn't protect anyone.

What if this had happened when someone was coming after her? He was pathetic. He was beyond help.

Addy deserved better. Once this passed, he'd tell her that. He'd find a way to get her another bodyguard. Even Phil was better than he was. Phil didn't fall to pieces because of a phone call.

It had been wrong of Rick to contact Addy's ex-husband; he knew that now. Deep down, he'd known it when he did it. He was so focused on not letting IronClad Elite shirk their responsibility that he couldn't stop himself. It was that moment the panic had started.

After another half hour, he was safe to drive. IronClad Elite had an office in Seattle. The fastest way to get to them would be by seaplane. He'd show up at the office, unannounced, and wouldn't leave until this was resolved. He wasn't much use to Addy, but if it was the last thing he did, he would get her more protection.

He put the car in drive. It was time to move.

. . .

The seaplane soared over the islands. He didn't need to see the view. Addy had already showed him.

Rick leaned back and closed his eyes. The adrenaline dump from the panic attacks always wore him out. He probably wouldn't have been safe to drive, and flying meant he could get to Addy more quickly.

He had to talk to her. As embarrassing as it was, he owed it to her to tell her what was going on. She needed to know the truth – the entire truth of how he'd failed.

She would probably try to minimize it, but Rick knew he wasn't good for anybody. He'd find a way to face her. Once he had a solution, it'd be easier.

They landed on Lake Union. The city was dull and gray, rain spitting now and then, flicking into his eyes. He texted his buddy and got the name of the top guy, then caught a ride to IronClad Elite.

After flashing his badge at the front desk, they let him through, no questions. He was too tired to answer questions.

The office was on the fourth floor. Right out of the elevator stood a shining desk in gunmetal gray. The floors and walls were coated in white marble. A woman with coifed hair and red lipstick smiled when she saw him.

"How can I help you?"

He held up his badge again. "I'm here to talk to Cliff."

She smiled, tapping something in her ear. "I'll see if he's available."

That was easy. Being authoritative worked. It was all fake, though. Everything he did was fake. Faking he was okay. Faking he knew what he was doing.

It'd be over soon. He could withdraw to a cabin somewhere. Have his panic attacks amongst the birds.

"He's coming now," the woman said with a smile.

"Thanks." His head was spinning with all these bright lights and reflective surfaces. He wanted to take a seat, but couldn't look any more weak than he was.

The door down the hallway opened and out walked a man with a rotund belly, greasy combover, and sagging eyes. His hands swung at his sides, weighed down with thick gold rings.

Rick blinked. He knew this guy. How did he know this guy?

"You looking for me?" he asked.

"Cliff?" Rick asked.

He nodded. "Who are you?"

It was him. The guy he and Addy met at the Flex Knock office. The one who watched them drive away with his belly pressed up against the door.

How was that possible? Was he losing his mind?

"My mistake," Rick straightened. "You weren't the Cliff I'm looking for."

He spun, pulled open the door to the stairs and tore off.

Twenty-six

The Lighthouse Bay office stood on the outskirts of town overlooking a gravel lot littered with decaying ships. There was no lighthouse, no bay.

The emptiness was spooky, but Addy had been smart about getting here. Joey had dropped her off at their usual spot, and she'd caught a ride with the unofficial cab guy who hung around the docks.

She pulled her hood over her head and walked on. If the cameras perched around were working, they'd have no way to trace her.

The ships stood like gravestones. Addy ducked cracked propellers and hopped over dislodged buoys until she reached the office.

The sign on the lopsided trailer read **LIGHTHOUSE BAY: YOUR INSURANCE STOP**. From the corner of her eye, she saw a camera perched above the door. Its light blinked red.

Addy pulled on the door. Locked. Hopefully that meant no one was inside.

She walked around the back and peered in the window. The lights were off. A fridge stood against the wall, and a chair sat askew from a brown desk.

Addy pushed on the window. It wouldn't budge. She tried the next two with the same result.

If Rick were here, he'd be able to pick the lock...

But Rick wasn't here. If he knew she were there, he'd be livid. Heat flashed up her face. What would she say? How could she excuse this?

Or worse—he wouldn't care at all.

Addy had to do this on her own. No one else thought it was worth it, but it was worth it to her.

Online, it said the office would be open. She thought she could distract whoever was working there and at least get a glimpse of the safe. Get an idea of what chance they had getting into it. She kept telling herself it wasn't stealing if she was taking back something that was hers – or, at least, her mom's. But the longer she stood in this eerie graveyard, the more it felt like stealing.

After half an hour of her poking around the trailer, the sound of seabird calls were interrupted by wheels on gravel. Addy stood, peering out from behind the building.

It was a white van. Her whole body got hot. Maybe it was time to go. This wasn't the way she'd wanted things to go.

The car stopped and the engine shut off. Addy strained to listen, peering around the edge of the trailer, the hood of her sweater obstructing part of her view.

"They forgot ketchup!"

Addy gasped, darting backwards. It was Julian. She thought she could hear Sebastian too, but she wasn't sure. Her throat tightened. Sweat poured down her back and chest. She hadn't expected to see them, but even more, she hadn't expected to be so afraid of them. Maybe her body understood something she didn't.

This plan would have to wait, or even be canceled entirely. She peered around again. They were arguing, their faces obscured by the van's open back doors. If she could just sneak out without them seeing her...

Addy moved swiftly, keeping her head down and sprinting toward the road. If she could just get past the trees, they wouldn't be able to see her.

Her foot caught, and she jolted to the ground. Addy slammed into the rocks, catching herself with her hands. Her bad shoulder screamed in pain.

"What the –"

Jaw clenched, Addy scrambled to her feet, stumbling forward, but it was too late. Footsteps pounded in her ears until both Julian and Sebastian were at her sides.

"Lookie what we have here!" Sebastian said, grinning.

"I'm just leaving," Addy said, pushing the hood off her head.

Julian stared with wide eyes. "Did you follow us here, you creep?"

Addy shook her head. "I came to get boat insurance."

Sebastian smirked. "Yeah, right. Do you want me to believe you got a magic unicorn too?"

She hated that smirk. "No."

"Sebastian," Julian said in a low voice, "you know what Cliff said."

"Yeah, but she showed up here herself."

She wrestled her arm out of his grip. "I'm going now."

Sebastian stepped in front of her. "You're not going anywhere."

He smelled of french fries and pickles. Addy cradled her arm. "Just let me go." She hated how her voice sounded pleading.

Sebastian shook his head, taking a deep breath as he stepped toward her. "I don't think so. I think we should talk."

She was quickly losing control of the situation. Rick would never have let this happen.

Whatever was going on, she couldn't let them bully her.

Addy drew herself up. "The way you talked to Judge Kearn?"

Julian smacked a hand to Sebastian's chest and muttered something in his ear.

"What do you know about that?" Julian said.

"Everything," she said, keeping her stare fixed.

"You're bluffing," Sebastian snapped.

She took a deep breath. It was like facing off with two hyenas. She couldn't show her fear. "I'm not. Now get out of my way or everyone will know just how much you paid the judge."

Julian shook his head. "Just let her go, man. We don't need to deal with this."

Addy's hand shook ever so slightly as she pulled her phone out of her pocket. "Should I call the police and tell them what I found?"

Sebastian slapped her phone to the ground. Julian bent to pick it up.

"Get out of here," Sebastian said. "Before I change my mind."

Julian walked off, back to the van. He pulled the door open and tossed her phone inside.

She hadn't expected that. Rick's voice ran through her head. Criminals don't think like normal people. They don't act like normal people...

"I better never hear from you again." Sebastian leaned in close, his sour breath hot on her face. "Or you won't be talking to anyone ever again."

Her mouth dropped open, and he laughed in her face. Then he and Julian turned and walked to the trailer. They unlocked the door before disappearing inside.

Addy stood there, holding her breath for what felt like minutes. She was afraid if she breathed, she might sob and get their attention.

She finally managed to take a shaky breath. This was quite possibly the dumbest thing she'd ever done. If she could just get out of here alive, she'd give this whole thing up. She'd never utter their names again, she'd wish her mom good luck. She'd move far, far away, out of their reach.

Her heart rate slowed. Maybe she could still get her phone so she could call for help. Call Joey. Sheila. Anyone.

Addy walked quietly to the back of the van and tried the door. It opened. She paused, looking at the trailer.

No movement. She had to work quickly.

Paint cans, old take-out containers. Tarps. A ladder. The front seats were separated from the back with a metal partition. It looked less like a murder van and more like a working van, albeit a messy one. She could do this.

She crawled inside, combing through the garbage until she found her phone wedged between a bucket and a toolbox. As she leaned forward to grab it, the door shut itself behind her

"Great," she muttered.

She pocketed her phone and shuffled back, pulling on the door handle.

Nothing but hollow resistance. She pushed, she kicked. The door wouldn't budge.

Addy shut her eyes.

No, *this* was the dumbest thing she's ever done. She was about to crawl to the front when the driver's door opened.

"He said they need the van," Julian sighed.

"Yeah, but we've got things to do," Sebastian said, climbing into the passenger seat.

Addy ducked down, covering her mouth with her hand. She was going for a ride.

Twenty-seven

This made no sense. Cliff, Flex Knock, IronClad Elite. There was no connection. There couldn't be.

And yet.

Rick got down to street level, his breath catching in his chest. No one had come after him, but his nerves were still fried from the morning. He needed a moment to think.

There was a coffee shop across the way. Coffee would help. Maybe decaf. Something hot, though.

He tossed a look over his shoulder before jogging over.

How was it possible that Cliff was in charge of IronClad Elite, yet he was associated – or maybe even in charge of? – the company that had come after Addy's mom?

He kept repeating it, over and over, trying to hold both ideas in his mind. When he thought too long about one, the other toppled out. It was impossible. He couldn't accept it.

The door to the coffee shop was eight feet tall and made from a stark, black metal. It was cool in his hands as he pushed it open.

The shop was local. No branding. No frills. The floors were a rich, earthy hardwood. The walls had canvases and framed pictures with price tags. Roasting beans drifted through the air. The jagged edges of his breaths evened out.

He ordered a decaf latte. Addy had put him onto lattes. She liked to get whipped cream on top.

He skipped the whipped cream. The barista served it in a round, nearly overflowing mug on a wide saucer. A pair of shortbread biscuits balanced on the edge.

Food. That was interesting. He was supposed to eat after the panic attacks. "I'm sorry," Rick said, pointing at the glass case, "can I also get one of those sandwiches?"

The barista nodded. "No problem."

He found a seat with a view of the door. No one had followed him. Had Cliff even recognized him? It seemed unlikely, but not impossible. Running out of there probably hadn't helped his case.

He pulled out his phone. Nothing from Addy. He hadn't expected her to talk to him after he'd disappeared like that. Rick shrank into his seat. She must think he was being unkind on purpose.

Not that he was losing his mind.

It was time to call her and tell her everything. If they were going to figure this out, they would figure it out together.

"Hi, you have reached Adelaide. I'm so sorry I missed your call... "

He hung up. She was probably angry at him. She had every right to be.

Rick hung up and typed out a text.

Hey, about earlier. I didn't want to leave. I had to, and I am so sorry. I'm coming back now and I'll explain every-

thing. I have something else I need to tell you, too. Please call me. It's important.

She would respond, even if she was angry.

In the meantime, he needed to reach out to his buddy about Cliff. Rick found his full name on the IronClad Elite website. He typed up an email between bites of sandwich, promising to repay the favor in any way if he could expedite the information.

It took about twenty minutes to pull together his email and send it out. By the end, there was still no word from Addy.

Rick shifted in his chair. A queasy wave hit his chest. Addy wasn't one to hold a grudge. It wasn't like she was on her phone all the time, but she was attentive. She said it was her duty as a mom, a habit she couldn't break.

He got up and cleared his table. It wasn't time to panic yet. He'd done enough panicking today.

By the time he stepped outside, his buddy had already answered. "I'll have this back to you in an hour."

It was good to have friends.

Rick caught a cab back to Lake Union and booked a return flight to San Juan Island.

Still nothing from Addy. He hated the panic attacks. They were humiliating and all-consuming but, on top of that, they threw him off. He didn't know when to trust his instincts. Was she in trouble? Was it instinct or more panic?

Something was off. He called the tea shop and Eliza picked up.

"Hey, is Addy around?"

"No, I haven't seen her all day. Is everything okay?"

"Ah, I hope so," Rick said, scratching the back of his neck. "I had some business in town and I haven't been able to reach her."

"Do you want me to run over to the house?"

He looked down at his hands. Was it unbelievable that a woman could be so angry at him that she wouldn't speak to him? Was he being paranoid, or was this real?

Rick didn't care if he seemed paranoid. All he cared about was Addy's safety. "If you don't mind."

"I'll call you back in five minutes!" Eliza said before clicking off.

Boats drifted on the lake. A yellow plane landed on the surface, then sputtered to a stop. Sailboats stood idly. There wasn't enough wind to move them.

Everything was painfully slow today. He tried to pull up Addy's location on his phone. It showed her as offline. Her last known location was in the middle of the ocean.

That didn't make sense.

His phone lit up. He grabbed it after one ring. "Hey."

"She's not at the house," Eliza said, breathlessly. "Joey was there, though. He said he flew her out to Bellingham. "

Ricks heart dropped. "Bellingham? For what? "

"He didn't know. Is that bad?"

Rick took a shaky breath. "Any time your aunt goes out to Bellingham, it's bad news."

Eliza laughed. "That's true."

"Can you tell Joey to hang around for a bit? I'm flying back to the island now, then I'll need a ride to Bellingham."

"No problem!"

He hung up. It was time to get onto the plane, but he needed to make one more call. "Mia, do you know where Addy is?"

"Uh, I might," she said slowly. "Aren't you with her?"

"I'm not." He heaved himself from the dock and into his seat. "I need to know where she is. She's not answering her phone."

"I'm so sorry!" Mia's voice cracked. "It was my idea."

"Tell me everything. I'm going to find her."

He slammed the plane's door shut. His mind was focused. He wasn't going to lose control again.

Twenty-eight

It was the longest ride of her life. Addy tried to find something to hold onto – the side of the van, a bucket full of paint – but as she moved, everything shifted and moved with her, bouncing over the bumps in the road.

The most she could do was try not to groan when they hit the biggest potholes at full speed.

They were terrible drivers. Terrible conversationalists, too. Her main focus was on being still and quiet, but she couldn't help but eavesdrop.

It didn't sound like anything intelligent: an argument over the best sauce for McNuggets; why Batman was the worst superhero; and which of them would survive time travel more readily.

And the music, if it even counted as that. It was loud and full of screaming, like cries out of her worst nightmare.

It didn't matter how terrible it was, though. It helped conceal her, even if it did give her a headache.

Mercifully, the car eventually stopped, and both men got out. Their bickering voices carried even after the doors shut.

Addy waited a minute before she dared to peek through the front window. She was in a parking lot surrounded by other cars. The sun was setting, the sky a mass of thick, charcoal clouds, swirling above like a shroud.

After another five minutes, she sat up and pulled on the metal partition separating her from the front seat.

It was no use. It was welded into place, probably to keep paint cans from flying and hitting them in their stupid heads.

She sank down, her hips aching, and pulled out her phone. More bad news. It had ten percent battery and no service.

She unlocked it anyway, the warm glow filling the space around her. There was a missed call from Eliza. A missed call from Rick, and two text messages.

Her heart leapt and she rushed to open them. The first one was long and cryptic. He apologized a lot, and said he had to tell her something.

What could that possibly be about? Here she thought he'd never speak to her again, and now there was something important she needed to know?

His second message was much shorter. "I am coming. Don't worry."

She smiled. There was no way he was going to find her, but she appreciated the thought. She tried to send him a message in return, but it wouldn't go through, spinning and spinning like a useless Ferris wheel.

She tried calling three times, but the ring wouldn't start.

Addy was in a dead zone. A total dead zone. She would probably be here for the rest of her natural life.

• • •

Her plan was simple. When Julian and Sebastian came back, hopefully in the morning, she would leap from the van and run as fast as she could. It was ridiculous, but her only chance at escape.

The hours of waiting wore her down. She tried to keep herself awake by envisioning the moment they returned. How she'd spring to action. How the wind would feel in her hair.

Yet other ideas floated in her head. What if she just rested her eyes for a moment? *Said no awake person ever.* Her eyelids fluttered shut and she drifted off, snapping back awake and scolding herself, then quickly drifting back into dreamland.

This process repeated for what she thought was minutes – until light blasted into the back of the van.

"Addy? Are you okay?"

She shot up, eyes wide, heart thundering in her chest. The sun was blindingly bright. She squinted, holding an arm to block the view.

So much for being alert and ready to run. She blinked and squinted into the light.

Her voice cracked. "Rick?"

Within seconds, he was in the back of the van, lifting her up. "Are you okay?"

His voice was more pressing now, his hand delicately breezing over her arm, her leg.

"I'm fine." She cleared her throat. It felt like she was floating, there in his arms, it felt like all the light was pouring out of her chest. She was more than fine, she was having a dream... "I'm not hurt."

They stood on black asphalt. He still had an arm around her, holding her steady. Addy's legs burned, blood rushing back like fire.

"I'm so sorry," he said. "I'm so sorry about everything. This never should've happened."

If it was a dream, she wasn't waking up.

"It's my fault," she said, waving a hand. "I got myself stuck in the van."

"I shouldn't have left you."

His eyes looked so pretty in this light. Addy grinned at him. "But you came back.'"

"Of course I came back."

The terror of the moment was gone. She was safe again. Addy tripped, falling into him. "That's all that matters."

"It's not," he said, steadying her. "You must be exhausted."

"I'm a little tired."

"Hang on a sec." He pulled out his phone. "Hey Mia, I've got her." A pause. "Yeah. Meet us at the gate."

Addy hobbled alongside him, letting her weight fall into his chest. This was far better than the plan she'd had. They worked better together. She closed her eyes for a moment, and it occurred to her she might still be asleep.

"Adelaide!" Mia shouted. She got out of her car, the engine still running, and threw her arms around Addy's neck. "I am so sorry I sent you in there alone!"

"I'm fine," Addy said. "Really. They took my phone, and when I tried to get it, I got stuck in the van."

"I am going to destroy both of them," Rick said quietly.

Mia and Addy exchanged glances.

"Are you hungry? I have some food in the car."

Addy shook her head. "No, I'm fine."

"Joey is waiting for us," Rick said. "We can fly back now."

"Thank you."

It was a short trip to the docks. Mia talked nonstop, guilt exploding from her. "I tried to find you. I went to the boat place, and it was so creepy, Addy! I got so scared, and then –"

Addy appreciated her concern, but it was getting harder to pay attention. Maybe she had managed to stay up for most of the night. Or maybe she just felt too sleepy around Rick.

She thanked Mia for her help and assured her she wasn't to blame. "This one's all on me," Addy said, giving her a hug.

Joey stood on the dock, doing a little hop when he saw them. "You found her!"

"I did," Rick nodded.

"How did you find me?" Addy asked, looking up at him.

"I'll tell you everything when we get back," he said softly. They took their seats and he spoke again. "Can I get you anything?"

"I might just rest my head on you if you don't mind..." Addy said.

She certainly wouldn't fall asleep with the loud engine, but she could at least rest her eyes. In seconds, she had drifted off again.

It was too bad she couldn't have held out a minute longer. She missed Rick whispering, "I've got you," before Joey started the engine.

Twenty-nine

The sun peeked from behind the house. The water was flat, and the air was filled with the chirping of birds as they carried out their important work.

Rick checked all the rooms in the house. Empty. Apparently Russell was tied up at the sea pen site, and Sheila was staying in Seattle to record her album.

He made a sandwich and cup of tea for Addy, then sent her upstairs to take a nap.

"I feel like I'm in trouble," Addy said with a laugh.

Rick shook his head. "You're not the one in trouble. I am. I'll tell you everything after you get some rest."

Surprisingly, she didn't argue. Rick sat on the floor outside her room until she emerged three hours later.

"It's sort of embarrassing," she said after she opened the door, her hair pressed to her forehead, her skin crossed with red creases. "To be sent away to nap like a baby."

"Not a baby. Like someone who was kidnapped."

She smiled and shook her head. "I wasn't kidnapped. I got trapped in the back of the van by my own accord."

He stared into her eyes. He'd thought he might never see them again. What a horrible world that would've been. If something had happened to her, he wouldn't have been able to live with himself.

"Would you like another cup of tea?" he asked.

"Tea would be great."

Downstairs, he put the kettle on and set out two mugs. It was time to confess. "I'm going to start from the beginning. I never should've taken this job. I wasn't fit to, and it was a selfish move."

Addy sat on a stool, her head slightly tilted. "What are you talking about? You're a great bodyguard."

He put a bag of chai into her mug, a bag of Earl Grey into his. "I wasn't honest with you. I didn't leave my last job because I was bored." He turned to face her, his arms crossed over his chest. "I was having events."

"What kind of events?" Addy asked.

"It started after I lost my cousin. Something would set me off and I couldn't breathe. My chest would get tight, and I thought I was going to die."

The tea kettle went off. He turned, pouring boiling water into her mug, then his.

"I thought something was wrong with my heart, but the doctor told me they were panic attacks." He set a timer for the tea. "I left my job after having one during a meeting. I can't tell you how embarrassing that was."

Steam rose up, circling and disappearing into the air. He turned, a mug in each hand, bracing for the horror on her face.

"Oh." Addy wrapped her hands around the mug. "That's nothing to be embarrassed about."

"When you're supposed to be in charge, it's very embarrassing. I kept losing control, and I felt like I was falling apart."

"I see," she said, slowly nodding. "But you still –"

He put up a hand. "I need you to know the full story."

She scrunched her shoulders and nodded.

"When a friend of mine offered me a position at IronClad Elite, I was desperate. I needed to prove I wasn't falling apart. I needed to prove I could still react, still protect someone. I was convinced if I could do that, then the panic attacks would stop."

Rick paused, rubbing his face with his hand. She was never going to look at him the same again, but it was for the best. She deserved to know.

He cleared his throat and went on. "I can't predict when they are going to happen, though, and when they start, I'm completely useless. It wasn't fair to you, it wasn't safe for you, and I am so sorry."

"No apology needed, Rick," she said quickly.

Of course she would say that. "When we argued yesterday, I felt a panic attack coming and I didn't want you to see. That's why I left." He lowered his eyes, focusing on his tea. "I left you vulnerable because I'm broken. I'm not fit to help anyone." He looked up, meeting her eyes. "I'm so sorry, Addy. I cannot express to you how sorry I am. If anything had happened to you..."

The timer went off. He took out the teabags and took a sip of tea. His throat loosened slightly with the burn.

She was quiet. Maybe she was deciding if she should yell at him. Scold him for putting her life in danger.

He deserved that, and more. He braced his grip on the counter.

She tapped his knuckles with her fingers. Her touch was as soft as rain.

"I have to disagree with some of the things you said," Addy said with a smile. "You're not falling apart. You're not broken. You're extremely capable, Rick. You found me in the back of that van, somehow."

He shook his head. "That never should've happened."

"Can I ask something?"

"Anything."

"What triggered your panic attack yesterday?"

He sighed. "It started when they told me the job was over. I felt the chaos coming on at the idea that you'd be unprotected. That was why I called your ex-husband. I didn't mean to disrespect you. I was desperate."

"Then, when he called and told me to grow up..."

"Yeah," Rick said. "That was when it fully hit. I couldn't think straight. I couldn't think of any other options."

She set her mug down. "What I'm hearing is that your panic attacks happen when you feel like you're out of control." She paused. "Not out of control, exactly. When you can't protect someone."

He looked into his mug. When he'd had a panic attack at work, it was right after getting a call about his mom. She'd called an ambulance, thinking she was having a stroke.

Then, another time, he was driving and saw a car veer off the road. He was useless then, too, trapped in his own car, unable to breathe. Unable to even call 911.

Rick shrugged. "I guess."

"It started after Cody passed away. When you decided you should've protected him," she added.

His chest hardened, his lungs like blocks of ice. He forced himself to take a breath. "Yeah. Maybe."

"I'm sorry. Did I cross a line?" Addy asked. "I didn't mean to. It just seems from the outside that –"

"No, you're right. I've thought about it, and how it didn't make sense, but it doesn't help. It doesn't stop the panic attacks. I thought if I could prove to myself that I wasn't useless –"

"You're not useless."

"I'm falling apart, Addy. I really am." He stared at her. It felt like his eyelids had picked up sand, grinding with every blink. "I'm no good for anybody."

"You may be falling apart, but that's not necessarily a bad thing."

This made him laugh, Addy's deluded optimism. He hadn't expected it to swing back around for him. "Oh, really?"

"When I was going through my divorce, I felt like I was falling apart, too. I was always anxious. Couldn't sleep. Couldn't eat. My head was jumbled. I was sure I was losing it."

He knew that feeling well.

She went on. "I used to get lunch with a friend at the university. He was a psychology professor, and he told me about a Polish psychologist, Kazimierz Dąbrowski. His theory was that inner turmoil isn't necessarily a sign of mental illness. He thought it could be a sign of growth."

Rick frowned. "This doesn't feel like growth."

"I know," Addy said with a laugh. "It feels like falling apart, because in a way, it is. He called it 'positive disintegration.' You break down, yes, but then you have the chance to put yourself back together. You become more emotionally complex, more mature."

"So you're saying," Rick said slowly, "that I'm Humpty Dumpty?"

A scowl crossed her face. "You and I both know all the king's horses and all the king's men couldn't put Humpty together again." A laugh burst out of her.

Rick found himself laughing too. "Is that not the case here?"

"You don't need the king's horses, or the king's men. You're putting yourself back together. You might be falling apart now, but you won't be falling apart forever. You're looking inward. You're coming back stronger. I promise."

He took a sip of tea. It had cooled, almost lukewarm now. "This doesn't change the fact that I should've sorted this out before I took on the job of protecting you."

"Eh." She waved a hand. "I disagree. We make a great team. Plus, it's not your job to protect me anymore. You got fired."

He nodded. "I sure did."

"Maybe you've been in the protector role for too long." Her eyes were fixed on him now. "Maybe you need a break."

He flinched. "I don't know about that."

"Sometimes an idea has been in our heads so long, we don't even think to question it. You don't have to protect everyone to be worth something, Rick. You're worthy just as you are."

"This is turning into a motivational speech."

Addy grinned. "I had a lot of time to think in the back of that van. I was trying to prove something, too...that I wasn't useless. Same word you keep repeating. I needed to show that I was worth something. More than what my ex-husband thought of me. More than what the world thought of me: an old, washed up, middle-aged woman."

"Of course you're worth something," he sputtered. "You're amazing, Addy. You're not old or washed up."

"But I am middle aged."

Rick smiled. "Aren't we all?"

She patted him on the hand. "You're still young. You'll find a way to put yourself together again, in a way that's not tangled with old ideas."

His chest floated, light and airy, the crushing weight drifting off like steam, disappearing into the air.

"I hope you're right."

She sat up straight. "I won't preach anymore. I'll give you a break. Plus, I need to know how you found me."

A smile pulled at his lips. This was much easier for him to talk about than the rest of that stuff.

He told her all about it – how once he had seen Cliff at IronClad Elite and gotten intel on him, he'd discovered Cliff was in charge of four other companies in the area, one of which was Lighthouse Bay.

That was the first place he'd checked after talking to Mia. He'd picked the lock at the trailer and watched the security footage. He'd watched footage of Addy walking around the Lighthouse Bay building and confronting the scumbags. Then, after seeing Addy disappear into the van, he checked the other two businesses in Bellingham.

The second one had the locked parking lot with the deserted van.

"It was easy, really," he said. "I'm just sorry I didn't find you sooner."

"I'm sorry I didn't wait for you! I wish I could pick locks," she laughed.

"Oh, right, about that." He walked over to the door and picked up a bag. "I found the safe in the trailer, but I couldn't open it."

"Ah. Bummer," she said.

"But the money wasn't in the safe. It was hidden at the bottom of a suitcase."

Her jaw dropped open. "No! Rick! You found it?"

He grinned. "I did. Well, most of it. I'm not sure how much is left." He dropped the bag on the kitchen island and unzipped it. "There's a lot of cash in there."

A white sheet of paper sat folded on top.

"That's my mom's handwriting!" Addy clutched at the piece of stationery with roses at the top. "This must've been her idea of a contract."

"Looks binding to me."

They erupted into laughter.

"I can't believe this," Addy said. "I can't believe *you*. You're amazing." She paused. "Even if you hadn't done any of this, you'd still be amazing."

He held up a hand. "All right, all right. I can't let this go to my head."

"I can't imagine it would." She shook her head. "This is unreal. I have something to tell you, too."

"Oh?" He settled into the seat next to her. He could listen to her talk for the rest of his life. "I'm all yours," he said.

Thirty

The story rolled out of her, like coins pouring into a fountain. Addy started from the beginning with the call from her husband. The things he'd said. How the words hit *just* the spot they needed to, pushing the buttons that sent her over the edge.

"I know it was stupid to do what I did," Addy said.

He held up a hand. "There's no judgment here. It wasn't stupid. It was human."

It was embarrassing that her ex-husband could still get to her like that. Then again, that was why he was her *ex*-husband.

She told him the rest: Mia's findings, how Flex Knock had paid off a judge, the text messages about the money being hidden away.

"I know there's more to this now," Addy said, tapping a finger on the counter. Her tea had gone cold, but she didn't need it. The blood pumping from her chest was red hot. "I can feel it in my bones. It's much bigger than stealing homes from desperate people."

"You're probably right," Rick said. "But what can we do?"

"I don't think *we* have to do anything." A grin spread across her face. She stood. "I feel like we're in a James Bond movie."

He laughed. "Oh?'"

"Yes! Aren't you a fan of Daniel Craig's Bond?"

"I have a hard time watching those movies," Rick said with a shrug. "It's too stressful."

"Oh, that makes sense." She nodded. There was nothing stressful to her about Daniel Craig's beautiful face, but she could see how that might not transfer to a war veteran. "Well, there's a running theme of the importance of work on the ground versus what you can get from behind a computer screen. Old verses new. You get the idea."

"Sure."

"And you just proved it! Mia's hacker was able to find a lot, but you found out more just by showing up at the IronClad office and seeing Cliff's stupid face."

Rick narrowed his eyes. "He does have a stupid face. Didn't like it from the first time I saw it."

"If we tell Mia's hacker what you found, I'm sure he can figure out even more. He can get to the bottom of all this."

"What do you think is at the bottom of all this?" Rick asked, tilting his head.

"I have no idea, but I can feel it's big." She bounced her shoulders with a squeal before practically running up the stairs.

"Hang on," Rick said. "I'm coming with you."

Addy spun around. "You don't have to be my bodyguard anymore. Sit here and relax."

"That's going to be a hard habit to break."

Her heart sank into her stomach. They were getting close to something. That she knew. She also knew that by unraveling this knot that had been around her neck, she would lose Rick forever.

Maybe she didn't want to talk to the hacker after all.

"You ready?" Rick asked, nodding toward the stairs.

It was no good to be selfish. He needed to move on with his life. She'd meant what she said. He was extraordinary. Kind, protective, considerate.

Handsome. She could admit it.

Just because her heart beat for him didn't mean she had a right to keep him here. There was more for him beyond her little world. He'd saved her life. Wasn't that enough? What more could she ask?

Addy knew the answer. Her little boring self had gotten far more than she'd bargained for. He'd opened her eyes. Called her bluffs. Made her question her own wrong ideas about herself.

She was lucky to have crossed paths with him. Most importantly, he made her feel like there was a chance she could be loved again.

"Yeah," she said weakly, taking the first step.

Thirty-one

One week. That was all Rick got before Addy connected all the dots and brought the whole operation crashing down.

The last panic attack felt like it had happened to someone else. He connected with a new therapist and had his first session virtually, the ocean at his back. He gave Addy more freedom, not insisting on following her around, but they still spent most of their time together. Drinking tea. Going to dinner. Going kayaking, again, this time trying to catch a wild orca pod swimming by. They were too slow, or maybe scared them off with their laughter booming across the water.

With the information Addy had found, the hacker was able to link Cliff to an organized crime family in California.

Rick wasn't shocked by this. Flex Knock and its underlings seemed shady from the first moment he laid eyes on them.

The rest of what the hacker uncovered shocked even Rick's weary soul.

Cliff worked under a company called Privatize Solutions. On the surface, it was a Canadian warehousing company with an interest in commercial real estate. The bland name hid a host of companies connected via personnel and funding – a telemarketing company that lied to people to fundraise; a cancer "charity" that absorbed ninety percent of donations for

administrative activities; a hedge fund that had lost the state of Pennsylvania's teachers pensions before folding up; a security company known as IronClad Elite; and, last but not least, the rapidly expanding business of home reorganization, Flex Knock.

Privatize Solutions also happened to be the company suing the Canadian government, arguing it was violating the Canadian Charter of Rights and Freedoms by limiting donations in political campaigns.

Rick about fell out of his seat when he heard that. This previously squeaky-clean company had brought the case Addy's husband was currently hearing.

She had debated if she should tell her ex-husband or go to the press. Ultimately, she did both. The mighty Judge Shane didn't seem interested in what she had to say until it became national news.

Mob Tied to Election Donation Lawsuit.

Only *then* did the honorable Judge Shane run with it. The reporters ripped the rest of the story apart, exposing the endless avenues of fraud and corruption from the organization and its goons. The public lambasted Privatize Solutions' plot to bring dirty money into Canadian politics, citing the disaster of repealing Citizen's United in 2010 in the US and allowing unlimited anonymous money to flow into politics.

For a solid seventy-two hours, it was the only story in the whole of Canada. Rather unfairly, Addy didn't receive any credit. The case was dropped, though, and that was enough for her.

"I don't want them knowing I figured it out," she argued. "They're dangerous people. We saw that. I don't want them thinking about me again."

Rick could only stare at her. "I know, but you put your life in danger to find this out."

She shrugged. "All in a day's work. "

He laughed. She was far too humble.

Back in the US, things were moving quickly, too. Cliff was arrested on racketeering charges. The Washington Attorney General brought a case against Flex Knock, and after a tip from an anonymous hacker citizen, both Sebastian and Julian had their parole revoked for separate violations.

The odd tragedy of it all was that Rick had no excuse to stay any longer. There was no threat left to Addy, and IronClad Elite still wanted their car back.

"I got a ferry ticket for tomorrow," he said weakly.

Her eyes fell. "Oh. Yeah, of course. You need to get back to your life. What do you think you're going to do next? "

"Nothing is going to live up to this job."

She grinned. "Sorry, buddy. You can't uncover an international scandal every week."

That evening, Addy went to the tea shop for one of Patty's famous tea parties. Mackenzie was on the island, and Marilyn and Lawrence were there to celebrate getting their money back.

Rick lagged behind to pack up his things. It was strange to be separated from Addy. It felt wrong, but he had to get used to it.

He thought it might trigger a panic attack, but it didn't. Instead, he wandered around, tidying things that didn't need to be tidied, staring longingly at places that held memories for him.

When the front door opened, he looked over with a leap in his heart, hoping Addy had come back for him.

Unfortunately, it was Marilyn.

"Hello, young Rick," she said, waltzing in, draped in a puffy red coat, the cuffs lined with feathers.

"Marilyn. It's nice to see you."

She took the coat off her slim shoulders and let it drop onto the couch. It feathered out as big as a blanket, draping over half the cushions. "I was afraid I wouldn't get a chance to thank you for what you did."

He looked down at his hands. "I was about to head over. I'm tidying up a few things."

"Tidying up a few things," she repeated, nodding. "I talked to Patty, you know."

There was nothing he'd like more than not to know. "That's nice."

She let out a huff. "You're not understanding me, Rick. I've come to do you a favor."

He raised his eyebrows. He had no interest in her favors. "Please don't worry about me."

Glass clanked and rolled. A wine bottle stopped at his feet.

"Remember this?" she asked.

Surely he hadn't shared a bottle of wine with Marilyn and blocked it out? Had she managed to drug him? "Can't say so, no."

She sighed, hands on her hips. "It's the bottle I caught Addy trying to throw into the ocean. You remember, the day we met?"

"Oh, sure. I'm pretty sure she was cleaning it up." And throwing out her shoulder. The memory warmed his chest.

"And *I'm* pretty sure I know my own daughter," she said. "You need to read the message inside and think about what you're doing. This is me thanking you. Got it?"

She picked up her coat and walked out, pausing to look over her shoulder. "I was never here." She winked a big, fake eyelash.

He watched as she shuffled back out the door.

His senses were really too dull to argue with her or ask what she was talking about.

Yet, despite thinking Marilyn was batty, he pulled out the cork. It took a minute of shaking for the note to fall out. He unraveled it and Addy's handwriting stared up at him.

It read simply, elegantly, in the middle of the page: *Will anyone ever love me again?*

His stomach lurched. What did that mean? How was Marilyn doing a favor for him by showing him this?

This seemed deeply personal for Addy. He shouldn't have opened it. But now, how could he ever forget?

Thirty-two

That morning, Rick wasn't outside Addy's door when she opened it. She'd have to get used to that. Get used to not seeing him, not laughing with him. Not making breakfast for him.

Maybe once he got wherever he was going, she could send him an email and see how he was doing. He might still want to talk.

No. She needed to wipe this silly fantasy from her mind and leave him alone. As kind as he was, as gracious as he'd been, this had been nothing more than a job to him.

It wasn't his fault her heart raced every time he walked in the room. He couldn't help that her dreams were haunted by his smiles.

It was just a crush. She'd get over it.

Okay, there was a chance it was more than a crush for her. He'd awakened something in the depths of her soul. For the first time, she thought her future could hold something more than loneliness. There was more to her than her past, and she actually wanted to keep going to see what that was.

Still, it was something to keep to herself. Not every revelation needed to be shared.

Rick was set to catch the morning ferry, and Addy wanted him to have one last egg sandwich before he left. She snuck down to the kitchen and melted clarified butter in the pan. She sliced the bread, not too thick, and popped it in the toaster. The coffee machine started its bubbling song, the aroma of roasted beans filling the air.

It had been nice, cooking for two. That was one thing that kept her from leaving the island. Russell and Sheila weren't always around, but it was good to have company. After so many years of marriage, being alone in an apartment was jarring. At night, she jumped at every sound. Addy left the TV on so it felt like someone else was there.

She wasn't ready to return to that life yet.

Rick came down the stairs just as she was putting his sandwich together.

"Good morning," she said, keeping her eyes on the cheese. Best to get it on there while the egg was hot. Melted cheese was key. "I'm not sure if you have time to eat this here, or if you'd prefer to take it with you. I wanted you to have something for the road, for old time's sake."

Old time's sake? Don't spoil what you've had by being a weirdo.

"I'm not going."

She looked up. He was wearing a black T-shirt, his muscles staring at her.

She looked back down. "I thought you had to return the car?"

Rick shook his head. "I had to do something else first."

He pulled an envelope from his back pocket and slid it across the kitchen counter.

"For me?" she joked, pulling up the flap.

Inside were two sheets of paper, both folded into thirds. Addy opened the first slowly, trying to process the words on the page.

A plane ticket to Naples. "Wow," she said softly, folding the paper back up. "You're going to Italy. You're going to love it."

"I hope so." He sucked in a breath. "There's another one there, actually."

Her eyes flashed to him, then to the second page. Another ticket, this one for Adelaide Ashbourne. Spots danced in her vision. The paper crinkled in her grip.

"I don't understand," Addy finally said.

Rick cleared his throat. "I have a confession. Last night, before I got to the tea party, your mom paid me a visit."

"My mom?" She shut her eyes. "I'm sorry. I shouldn't have told her you found her money."

"I'm glad you did. She gave me the wine bottle you had the first day we met. I'm not proud of this, but she said some things that led me to look inside. At the, ah, message. In the bottle."

Addy's hand flew to her mouth. How had she forgotten about that note? "That was a whole thing about this book I was reading, and it's really embarrassing –"

"It's not embarrassing. Nothing about it is embarrassing." He smiled that adorable half smile. "You kept talking about how amazing I am. What about how amazing *you* are? You're intelligent, beautiful. Brave."

She laughed. "Brave, or –"

"Brave," he said firmly. "You spent so many years not being seen by your ex-husband. Well, Addy, I see you. All of you, and I'm crazy about every part. I don't ever want to be away from you, and not in the bodyguard way. In the you-make-me-happy-to-wake-up way. In the you-inspire-me-to-become-a-better-person way." He paused. "The you-make-life-worth-living way."

Her vision clouded with tears. "I feel like I'm hallucinating."

He laughed, and Addy did too, tears spilling down her cheeks.

"I get that. I can't feel my limbs," Rick said. "I would guess it's a panic attack, but I know it isn't, because you're here."

She grabbed his hand. "Rick..."

"It doesn't have to be Italy. It can be anywhere. Anywhere with you."

A ball formed in her throat and she could barely speak past it. "I'd like that very much."

A smile spread across his face. "Really?"

She jumped, wrapping her arms around his neck. "Yes!"

He caught her, lifting her up, pulling back to look at her face. "I'm so glad I asked."

Then he kissed her. She closed her eyes, and she wasn't sure if it was the lack of oxygen to her brain, or if there really were stars exploding in every inch of her chest.

Epilogue

After a week, Mia couldn't take it anymore. She broke down and called her dad.

He answered with a far too bright tone. "Hey, Mia!"

He had no choice but to sound happy to hear from her with all that unconditional love he had.

Mia sighed. "Hi, Dad."

His tone shifted. "Is something wrong?"

"Well, I got Addy kidnapped. Is she still upset?" She dropped her voice. "Is Sheila upset?"

"What? No!" He laughed. "Is that why you've been avoiding my calls?"

She'd said she was busy. It wasn't a total lie. She was busy feeling guilty, imagining all the ways it could've gotten worse. "Yes."

"I promise you, no one is angry. They have no reason to be. Adelaide took matters into her own hands, and she's very happy with how things turned out. You didn't hear?"

Mia frowned. "No. I didn't hear anything."

"I know she's been meaning to call you – it's been hectic. How about Joey picks you up and you talk to her yourself?"

She bit her lip. "Is Rick still there?"

"He is, and he's not upset either. Please, come on. I'd love to see you. Eliza's making apple cobbler. She serves it on home-made vanilla ice cream."

Hm. Staring at the brown walls of her apartment or eating hot, cinnamon-soaked apples as they melt into homemade ice cream?

"Okay," she finally said. "It'd be nice to see you, too."

"There's my girl!"

Two hours later, she was in the seaplane making an approach on San Juan Island.

"What have I missed?" Mia asked over her headset.

Joey turned to her with wide eyes. "Tons of stuff. Are you kidding me?"

He rattled off a list of discoveries Addy and Rick had made after the kidnapping, connecting Flex Knock to corruption all the way in Canada.

"That is insane!" Mia said, shaking her head.

"Oops." Joey made a face. "Addy probably wanted to tell you that herself. Try to act surprised when she tells you."

They descended, circling a spot to land. The weight on her chest lifted. "I will."

Inside the tea shop, all was calm. Sheila and Addy sat at a corner table, eyes focused on their computer screens. Eliza was just disappearing into the kitchen, and Russell was off to the side with Rick.

Joey yelled hello as he pushed the door open.

"I'm back here!" Eliza called out.

He grinned, disappearing behind the swinging door.

Mia quietly snuck up on Addy's table and reached the edge before she spoke. "Hi."

Addy looked up and a smile spread across her face. "Mia!" She stood and pulled her in for a hug.

"Hey there!" Sheila said, taking her turn.

Mia finished hugging everyone and stood back, shoulders squared. "Addy," she said heavily, "I have been thinking about this nonstop and I have to tell you I am so, so sorry about what happened. I have no excuse for letting you get kidnapped. It's been turning in my head how badly it could've gone, and I just can't sleep. I let myself get too caught up the excitement and –"

Addy put up a hand. "No Mia, I'm sorry! I haven't had time to catch you up on everything."

Mia dropped her voice. "Joey told me on the way over. Though he told me not to tell he told."

"Oh, good!" She laughed. "There's nothing to be sorry about. You were key to piecing that mystery together. You were amazing! Besides, I'm an adult and I make my own bad choices."

Rick walked over and put his arm around her shoulders. "There's the truth. She's unstoppable."

Mia blinked at them.

Rick narrowed his eyes. "Nice to see you too, little hacker."

"I'm not the hacker," Mia said, "but hang on... uh, did I miss something?"

Addy and Rick looked at each other and smiled.

Mia turned to look back at her dad.

He cupped his hands around his mouth and yelled, "They're madly in love."

Addy rolled her eyes. "Thanks, Russell."

"When did this happen?" Mia shouted. "Joey forgot to mention that."

"He's a terrible gossip," Sheila said with a sigh. "And by that, I mean he's terrible at it. Always leaving out the good parts."

"I guess it all happened after I got trapped in that van." Addy shrugged. "So, in a way, this is all your fault."

Mia's hands were on her face, her mouth hanging open. "I'm so happy for you!"

"Thank you." Addy beamed. "If you can excuse me for a second, I need to go check on Patty."

"I'll come with you," Rick said.

Sheila walked over and bumped Mia with her hip. "I've never seen Addy so happy."

"I'm so happy for her. Rick is so kind."

Sheila nodded. "And so cute."

"So cute!" Mia agreed.

Russell walked over. "Excuse me, I thought I was cute?"

"You are, dear," she said. "Don't worry."

Mia chortled a laugh. "Okay, Dad, no need to be jealous."

"I'm not jealous. I could whisk Sheila off to Italy."

She shook her head. "Don't you dare. We don't have time for that."

He sighed and turned to Mia. "I'm not allowed to be romantic."

"When are they going to Italy?" Mia asked.

"Next week. Addy wanted to visit her daughter Riley first. Riley is very keen to meet the mysterious Rick and she's excited for her mom."

The weight on Mia's chest was entirely replaced by a warm and cozy pot of tea. "That's so sweet."

Russell nodded. "It was your best kidnapping yet. I don't know if you can top it."

Mia rolled her eyes. "I think I'll retire while I'm on top."

"Good idea."

Her phone buzzed in her pocket. Mom.

She slipped outside to take the call. "Hey Mom! Everything okay?"

"Everything is great! How are you?"

"I'm good. Visiting Dad on San Juan Island."

"Oh, nice." She sighed. "I really miss you. I'm going to come visit as soon as this shoot is over."

"I'd love that. I miss you too."

"I have something else to tell you. Something to look forward to."

"Oh?" Mia took a seat on the picnic table looking over the sea. Her view from her apartment was of a parking lot and a dumpster. Her dad had her beat here. If Addy and Rick were going off to travel, he might have an opening in his house soon...

"I know you've been having a hard time with the press and the critics after your last movie," her mom said slowly, "and I think I might have found a solution."

"For me to quit acting?" Mia said with a laugh.

"No! Of course not. Never give up. Never ever give up." Her mom cleared her throat. "There's a new movie. I was approached by this incredible director who wants to shoot an indie film with a mother and daughter pair. He said the first people he thought of were us."

Mia's stomach leapt. "Well, that's very flattering."

"I agree. It would be a quick shoot. You'd have a number of key scenes, but there aren't as many as your last movie, so you'd have time to work through them. Make the character exactly how you want her to be."

It was temping, but... "I don't know, Mom. I think I've embarrassed myself enough."

"I'm not going to pressure you into it. I want to send you the script. Read it over. It made me think of that actress, you know, Margaret Qualley? She did that amazing show with her mom and everyone loved it!"

Mia laughed. "She's a good actress, though."

"You're a good actress, too! And we could spend so much time together on set! I could help coach you – if you wanted that, of course. We could work together and it would be so much fun."

"It would be really fun to work with you." Mia bit her lip.

What did she have to lose? Being even more embarrassed? Was that even possible?

"It'll be a low budget, small film, so if it doesn't go anywhere, I don't expect you'll have people hounding you again. If it takes off, then your career will finally be where it was meant to be."

Oh, a mother's unfaltering love. Mia couldn't help but laugh. "I don't know what to say."

"Say yes!" Mom paused. "Or at least say you'll think about it."

"I don't know who I'm kidding," Mia said. "I don't have any other opportunities right now and that sounds really fun so...yes!"

Her mom squealed. "Yes! I'll send it over right now. I love you, honey!"

"I love you too, Mom."

Mia hung up the call and took a deep breath. The sun sparkled on the water and warmed her face. The air was cool on her skin. It was a perfect day in a perfect place, enough to make Mia believe that even she could have a new beginning.

She stood, casting one last glance at the sea, before walking back to the tea shop. When she pulled the door open, laughter poured out to greet her.

The Next Chapter

Introduction to *A Spot of Summer*

A famous actress, a divorcé, and a popstar walk into a (sand)bar...

All Mia Westwood was looking for on San Juan Island was a relaxing place to await the release of her latest film. Instead, she found friendship with a popstar, a perplexing mystery, and romantic feelings for a newly divorced island native who is not ready for a relationship. Seems like a story only Hollywood could've scripted, right? If only...

Jacob Kowalski just wanted peace and quiet after his devastating divorce. But how was he supposed to get that when a beautiful, headstrong woman with big city connections kept inserting herself into a high profile investigation...and his every waking thought?

It's not long before Mia and Jacob's attraction grows into something much more complicated—especially since Mia's only in town for a short time and Jacob's roots are firmly planted on the island. But when all is said and done, can they turn their summer romance into a happily ever after?

A Spot of Summer, book five in the Spotted Cottage series, is a contemporary women's fiction novel with plenty of sweet romance, small-town charm, and a delightful cozy mystery. Get your copy now, and welcome to the island!

Reader's Newsletter

Want to dive deeper into the Spotted Cottage Series?

Sign up to Amelia's newsletter and get bonus content from the entire Spotted Cottage series including:

- Rick's postcard to Addy
- Recipes from Eliza and Patty
- A bonus chapter with Sheila and Russell's first Christmas

Visit https://mailchi.mp/0548bfa882d1/rick to get your copy now!

About the Author

Amelia Addler writes always sweet, always swoon-worthy romance stories and believes that everyone deserves their own happily ever after.

Her soulmate is a man who once spent five weeks driving her to work at 4AM after her car broke down (and he didn't complain, not even once). She is lucky enough to be married to that man and they live in Pittsburgh with their little yellow mutt. Visit her website at AmeliaAddler.com or drop her an email at amelia@AmeliaAddler.com.

Also by Amelia...

The Spotted Cottage Series

The Spotted Cottage by the Sea
A Spot of Tea
A Spot at Starlight Beach
Spotted at Lighthouse Bay
A Spot of Summer

The Westcott Bay Series

Saltwater Cove
Saltwater Studios
Saltwater Secrets
Saltwater Crossing
Saltwater Falls
Saltwater Memories
Saltwater Promises
Christmas at Saltwater Cove

The Orcas Island Series

Sunset Cove
Sunset Secrets
Sunset Tides
Sunset Weddings
Sunset Serenade

www.ingramcontent.com/pod-product-compliance
Lightning Source LLC
Chambersburg PA
CBHW031444200726
48289CB00007BB/2199